LILY

A Screenplay by

Livia Milano

Livia Milano, Publisher | Berkeley 2021

This book is dedicated to my beautiful-on-the-inside-and-outside daughters Julia Milano and Cassidy Milano. I am eternally grateful to be your mom and forever in awe of your kind hearts and passion for life. Thank you for making me a better person. I love you to the moon and beyond always.

INTRODUCTION:

Livia Milano is mother to Julia Milano (Civil Engineer) and Cassidy Milano (UC Berkeley College Student). Livia majored in Film Production at Chapman University and went on to get a BA in Cinema/TV Arts from California State University, Northridge and an MA in Mass Communication with an emphasis in Screenwriting. Livia is a Sag-Aftra Actor, Writer, Podcaster and Stand Up Comedian. She is best known for her stint on Millionaire Matchmaker (3 times), but is more proud of her role as a $10 crackwhore opposite Nick Stahl and Rose McGowan in the film *Dead Awake.* Livia made her stand up comedy debut in the Belly Room at the Comedy Store in 2011. She launched *The Not So Sexy, Sexy Podcast with Liv Milano* in January 2019 which has ranked in the top 200 of comedy podcasts on Apple Podcasts and in the top 10 in the Stand Up category in the US and worldwide. Livia is a 1st generation Italian-American and according to Ancestry.com, is 100% Southern Italian.

Lily is a wacky, hilarious and heartwarming tale about an Italian-American family navigating old-country-Italian ways in modern day Los Angeles. Lily, the daughter and protagonist, believes she has been cursed at birth by a Witch in Italy to punish her mother, Michela, who conceived out of wedlock and broke the family tradition of caring for her mother until death. Lily lives a life of hexed mayhem and longs for independence from her family's old-fashioned values. A little person nemesis, a Studio City psychic, over-protective brothers, a clueless father, a highly superstitious mother and a boy-band love interest provide lots of chaos and fun as Lily adventurously carves out her own path in life. Lily goes from a self-loathing disaster to a loyal friend all while breaking her mother's heart.

FADE IN:

INT. BEDROOM IN ITALY - NIGHT

MICHELA, age 28, lays in bed and sobs in a corner of the room. She just gave birth. MIMMO, age 30, her boyfriend, slumps over her and tries to comfort her. CARMELLA (Michela's Grandmother) wears a black dress, gray hair in bun, holds a rosary.

At the foot of the bed (which is draped by a sheer red cloth hung from the ceiling), the NEWBORN (LILY) is held by Michela's Mother LUCIA. Lucia has waist length gray hair and wears a structured black dress. SEBA, the country WITCH, stands next to Lucia. She wears a black scarf over her curly gray hair and holds a large wooden crucifix.

The room is lit by kerosene lanterns. The year is 1966, but the village is old country Italy without regular electricity. Dark red curtains with gold trim align the many windows in the room. Gold damask wallpaper coats the walls. A statue of the Virgin Mary is on a bedside table surrounded by red candles.

Speech of characters in ITALIAN.

LUCIA (loud): *Michela, hai infranto la tradizione e hai svergognato la tua famiglia e per questo la tua figlia neonata soffrirà.* Michela, you have broken the tradition and have shamed your family and for this your newborn daughter shall suffer.

MICHELA (sobs): *No mamma per favore! È una bambina innocente.* No Mama please! She is an innocent child.

LUCIA: *E tu Mimmo, anche tu sei da biasimare. Li porti entrambi fuori da casa mia entro mattina. Non verrò al matrimonio e non vedrò più nessuno di voi.* And you Mimmo, you are also to blame. You take both of them out of my house by morning. I will not come to the wedding nor see any of you again.

MIMMO: *Non provi compassione, tua figlia soffre. Il dottore ha detto che ha bisogno di dormire.* Have you no sympathy, your daughter is in pain. The doctor said she needs bed rest.

LUCIA: *Non ha simpatia per me. È la mia figlia più giovane e avrebbe dovuto prendersi cura di me finché non sarò morto. Ora esci di casa prima che chiami la polizia.* She has no sympathy for me. She is my youngest daughter and was supposed to care for me until I'm dead. Now get out of my house before I call the police.

Mimmo strokes the sweat off Michela's face with a kerchief.

MIMMO: *Amore mio, sarò qui per prima cosa domattina e prometto di darti una vita piena di felicità in America.* My love, I will be here first thing in the morning and I promise to give you a life full of happiness in America.

MICHELA: *Ti amo.* I love you.

MIMMO: *Ti amo di più.* I love you more.

Mimmo kisses her forehead and she closes her eyes. She winces in pain. He gives Carmella a hug and knows that he will never see her again. He puts his head down and walks out the door.

Carmella tears up and begins to CHANT the prayers of the rosary. Seba sets down the large cross and Lucia hands the baby to Seba, the witch. Seba is dressed like a Gypsy. She dips one hand into her apron pocket and coats her finger in black ash. She makes an upside down cross on Lily's forehead.

SEBA (sings): *La tua vita sarà maledetta dal malocchio.* Your lifetime will be cursed with the evil eye.

Lucia pours water into a bowl and cleanses her hands as if the baby was germ infested.

MICHELA: *Non ascoltare, Lily. Vai a dormire bambina.* Don't listen, Lily. Go to sleep baby.

SEBA: *La sfortuna ti circonderà. La tua visione della vita deve essere pessimista.* Bad luck shall surround you. Your outlook on life shall be pessimistic.

Carmella CHANTS the rosary louder. Lucia still frantically washes her hands.

SEBA: *La tua vita sarà piena di tormenti e frustrazioni. Pagherai per i peccati di tua madre.* Your life will be full of torment and frustration. You will pay for your

Mother's sins.

MICHELA: *Che tipo di madre sei tu che faresti questo a tua figlia?* What kind of mother are you who would do this to your own daughter?

Seba closes her eyes as if she is in a trance. Lucia ignores her and manically scrubs her hands.

Michela grabs the statue of the Virgin Mary from her bed and throws it at her mother. It misses and CRASHES to the floor. Everyone is shocked and a moment of silence.

LUCIA: *Non solo sei una vergogna, sei malvagia. Ora dormi con il tuo bambina e prega per il perdono.* Not only are you a shame, you are evil. Now sleep with your baby and pray for forgiveness.

Lucia motions for Seba to give her the baby. Seba and Lucia pick up the pieces of the statue.

CARMELLA (whispers): *Non preoccuparti bambina. Mimmo è un brav'uomo e si prenderà cura di entrambi. Ora dai da mangiare alla tua Lily. Pregherò per tutti voi.* Do not worry child. Mimmo is a good man and will take care of you both. Now feed your Lily. I will pray for all of you.

Lucia and Seba carry the broken pieces of the Virgin Mary out of the room. A shard of it pierces Lucia's hand and her hand bleeds. She gives Michela one last look of shame on her way out.

Michela begins to nurse the baby. Lily's big eyes look

frightened as she eats. Carmella takes out a pocket knife and tears a hole into the bottom side of the mattress. She pulls out a wad of American hundred dollar bills and another stack of Euros and hands and opens a seam in the handmade blanket where she puts the money. She sews it up with a needle from the nightstand drawer. Carmella pinches Michela's cheek and they share a warm smile.

EXT. OCEAN - NIGHT

A ship sails in a rough sea. It begins to rain. It is dark and you can barely see the ship until the lightning flashes. Thunder rumbles and the haunting sound of waves slap the side of the ship.

EXT. OCEAN - DAY

Mimmo, Michela and their baby Lily stand on the deck of the ship in calm waters. They embrace and stand tall as the ship slowly sails into New York with the Statue of Liberty in the distance.

DISSOLVE TO:

EXT. BIRDS EYE VIEW OF LOS ANGELES - DAY

Italian, ACCORDION music plays as we see the city of Los Angeles and the coast down below.

TWENTY YEARS LATER is in captions.

INT. WHITE BUICK - MOMENTS LATER

Mimmo pulls up in a white buick. The music stops as he gets out of the car, but he still SINGS.

INT. LILY'S ROOM - MOMENTS LATER

A collection of butterflies in box frames align her cranberry colored walls. Brightly colored bean bags form a circle next to her bed. Her bookshelf is filled with books about Italy and a globe collection of different sizes. Red and gold beads hang in her doorway. LILY (21) an Italian cutie(adorned in a head full of curls) awakens to the sound of her brothers and mother SCREAMING at each other.

INT. KITCHEN - MOMENTS LATER

Michela wears an apron and kneads dough. Lily's younger brothers VINNIE (17 looks like a greaser straight out of the movie Grease) and JOEY (16 a little plump and does not look like his Italian family at all) sit at table and eat pieces of fried dough with butter and sugar (doughboys).

The kitchen is filled with brass pots that hang from the ceiling. A small orange radio is blaring the same Italian song that Mimmo had in the car. Mimmo and Michela speak in a broken Italian/East Coast accent.

VINNIE: You stupid fuck, you completely ruined my chances with Angie!

JOEY: How am I supposed to know she didn't know about Cynthia!

MICHELA (overlapping): That's enough!

VINNIE: Ma, you don't understand...

JOEY: I can't keep track of all of your sluts.

VINNIE: Angie wasn't a slut she was a nice girl.

JOEY: Then I did her a favor, she doesn't belong with a scumbag like you anyway.

MIMMO (overlapping): Oh, Oh, Oh! Don't you ever let me hear you disrespecting women in the presence of your mother. What's the matter with you?

MICHELA: Where do you think they learn it from?

MIMMO: It's gonna start this early, I thought we could wait until I at least had my breakfast.

MICHELA: Well you're late anyway. Here, eat.

Michela puts a doughboy on the table for him.

MIMMO: That's it. I can't eat.

VINNIE (to Joey): You know, you're a fucking prick!

MIMMO: Shut up!

All of a sudden, Lily SCREAMS from upstairs. Everyone runs out of the kitchen.

INT. LILY'S ROOM - MOMENTS LATER

Lily stands on her bed wrapped in a blanket and frantically ducks from a black bird that darts at her head. Her family runs into the room. Pure chaos. There is a hole in the screen of the window. Her mother swishes her apron at the bird. Mimmo grabs a life size barbie doll and tries to swing it at the bird. Joey pushes Vinnie toward the bird and laughs and the two get into a childish slap fight.

MICHELA (in Italian): God damn it, mother of God, what the hell is going on?

The boys slam into their father and practically knock him off his feet.

MIMMO: This is a crazy house. I can't take it anymore.

Michela continues to CURSE in Italian.

MICHELA: When a bird comes in the house, it means someone is going to die!

Michela bursts into tears.

MIMMO: God damn it Michela, shut up. Joey and Vinnie out!

Lily peeks her head out of the blanket as the bird flies straight toward her face. Lily SCREAMS.

MIMMO: Wait! I've got him!

Mimmo prepares the life size barbie like a bat and swings full force at the bird. He misses the bird and clocks Lily right in the face. Lily flies off the bed and lands on her back. Everyone stands around her in shock.

The black bird flies out the window.

JOEY (laughs): Holy shit!

INT. HOSPITAL - LATER

Lily lays in a cot in the emergency room enclosed by a white curtain. A heart monitor is next to her bed and makes odd NOISES. Her entire family stands around her bed. DR. RONALD (35) checks her heartbeat. He wears a bright, paint splattered smock. His hair looks like a curly mushroom. He wears glasses that are much too big for his face and has a bushy mustache. His manners are slow and creepy, but they've known him for a long time.

DR. RONALD (hesitant): Your heartbeat is a pleasure to hear as usual. Let me put some ointment on that badboy...

Points to the swelled up gash on her forehead.

DR. RONALD: And you should be fine. Don't worry a little swelling won't distract from your perfectly round, beautiful eyes and lips so sweet...

MIMMO: Alright alright so she'll be fine, that you very much Dr. Ronald.

MICHELA (infatuated): Mimmo, let him finish, he wasn't finished.

MIMMO: Finish what? He said she's gonna be fine.

MICHELA: Yeah, next time maybe she won't be.

MIMMO: God damn it, it was an accident.

VINNIE: Ma, give me a dollar. I want to go get a chocolate bar.

JOEY: What's the matter, Angie won't bang you any-more?

VINNIE: Oh you're so funny. Because chocolate is like sex. Shut up you stupid son of the milk man.

JOEY: Ma!!!

Michela grabs a handkerchief out of the sleeve of her shirt and acts like she's going to hit Vinnie with it.

LILY: Shut up, all of you!

An awkward silence.

DR. RONALD: Lily if you need anything at all, here's my house number. Oh and here's my cell phone and I might as well give you the number to where I play bingo. Just in case.

Mimmo grabs the piece of paper out of the doctor's hand and shoves it in his shirt pocket.

MIMMO (to Lily): Let's go. You'll live.

INT. DINING ROOM - EVENING

Michela walks in and out of the dining room with different foods like: spinach pie, arugula salad, spaghetti, cutlets, etc. Her apron is a mess with flour in her hair. Everyone sits around a circular table. Lily is in between her two brothers. Everyone digs in before all of the food arrives and before Michela sits down she does the sign of the cross.

Two conversations go on simultaneously between

Joey and Vinnie and between Mimmo and Michela. Lily sits in silence and eats spaghetti. She has a big bandage on her forehead.

VINNIE: Did anyone call?

MIMMO: Michela, where's the meatballs? You know I can't eat spaghetti without meatballs.

JOEY: I don't know, how much is it worth to you?

Michela YELLS from the kitchen.

MICHELA (O.S.): I put the meat in the sauce this time!

VINNIE: Very funny. Who called Milkman?

MIMMO: You did what?

JOEY: I can't remember.

MICHELA (O.S.): I put the meat in the sauce!

She walks over to his plate and points to the ground beef.

VINNIE: Well maybe if I shove this fork up your ass, your memory will improve.

MIMMO: That's the lazy way. I can't eat this.

JOEY: Or maybe you can lend me your mustang after dinner.

MICHELA: Lazy? I made homemade spinach pie all morning. I was tired. You make the meatballs.

VINNIE: Why do you need the car?

MIMMO: Oh okay. And you go to work in the morning. Oh yeah and the car needs a new transmission, how about you fix that too.

Lily twirls her spaghetti completely unaffected.

JOEY: I'm going out with Sarah? Come on.

MICHELA: You know what, don't eat!

Mimmo grabs the salad bowl defeated and starts to eat out of the large bowl quietly.

VINNIE: Oh my god, you mean Sarah Sarah? She's fatter than you. You're gonna make fat babies.

JOEY: At least she has a good personality. Come on you jerk. Can I borrow the car or not?

VINNIE: Yeah now who called?

JOEY: The keys.

Vinnie takes the keys out of his pocket and drops them in his glass of water.

JOEY: Angie called and she wanted me to tell you that you're a cheating son of a bitch and she fucked Nick. Isn't that your best friend?

Vinnie is visibly upset but tries to keep his cool. Michela runs into the kitchen again.

MIMMO: Why don't you sit down and eat? What's the matter with you?

MICHELA: I forgot my fork.

Michela sits down finally.

MICHELA: Happy Birthday Lily.

MIMMO: Oh it's your birthday? Happy Birthday. How old are you now, eighteen?

LILY: I'm twenty-one dad.

MIMMO: Oh that's right, twenty-one.

Her brothers are on each side of her at the table and give her a kiss on the cheek.

JOEY AND VINNIE: Happy Birthday Lily.

MICHELA: I made you a carrot cake, your favorite.

LILY: Lady finger cake is my favorite Ma, but thank you.

MICHELA: Oh. Can't please anyone tonight.

VINNIE: Joey no funny business in the back seat of my car. You understand?

Joey rolls his eyes.

MIMMO: I can't eat this. I thought I was gonna have meatballs tonight.

He pushes the salad bowl away. Joey gets a text. Looks disappointed.

JOEY: Nevermind she cancelled.

VINNIE: Good. I don't need you getting your cherry popped in my car.

Joey takes a huge bite of bread. Mimmo pushes the salad bowl away.

MIMMO (to Lily): So what are you gonna do now that you're twenty. Not a teenager anymore.

LILY: I'm moving out.

Michela bursts into tears. Mimmo gets up, slams his fork down and walks out. Her brothers stare at her and laugh. Lily takes another bite of her spaghetti.

CUT TO:

INT. PARENT'S BEDROOM - MORNING

Lily walks in with her hair up in a scarf and a backpack slung over her shoulders. Mimmo smokes a cigarette in bed. An ashtray overflows on the nightstand. Michela is asleep.

MIMMO: You know you're ruining your mother.

LILY: Dad, I just came to say goodbye. Ma, wake up.

MICHELA (suddenly awake): What?

LILY: Here, I got you something.

MICHELA: What is it? I don't want it.

LILY: It's nothing. Just open it.

Michela unwraps the gift of a small statue of the virgin Mary. Lily smiles.

MIMMO: Uh-oh.

MICHELA: You got me a statue of a saint?

Michela starts to CRY and overreact.

MICHELA: She's trying to kill me!

LILY: What are you talking about?

MICHELA: You know you're never supposed to give a statue of a saint as a gift, it's bad luck!

LILY: Oh just like the knife set I got you last Christmas that you made me pierce you with like a crazy person.

MICHELA: You never give sharp objects. It means you will be enemies. You had to draw blood. It's the only way to break the curse.

LILY: There's no curse Ma!

MICHELA: You had to do that or we would have been enemies. There's no way to undo this curse.

Michela is distraught. Mimmo takes the statue and puts it in the nightstand drawer.

LILY: Jesus Christ Mom, I can't keep up with all of your superstitions.

MICHELA (to Mimmo): Did you hear that? She is taking his name in vain.

Mimmo puts his arm around Michela and tries to comfort her.

LILY: That's it I can't take it anymore. Dad treats you

like shit. Joey and Vinnie are disgusting pigs who talk about sex nonstop, but heaven for bid if I say Jesus Christ!

MICHELA: I said don't say that!

Michela signs the cross.

MICHELA: She's trying to kill me!

LILY: I always thought that I was the crazy one, but you're all nuts and I'm leaving. Goodbye!

Lily storms out of the room and slams the door behind her.

MIMMO: Get back here! You're never gonna make it on your own.

Lily opens the door again just to scream back.

LILY: For your information I have a job and 2 months of rent saved and I am gonna make it!

MIMMO: What, you have $2000?! $2000! You're gonna come back home and I know it. You can't do it. You're a girl!

Lily is so angry and SLAMS the door.

INT. ISUZU TROOPER - LATER

Soothing meditation MUSIC blares from Lily's car stereo. Her windows are all down and her long, black hair blows freely in the wind. She drives through a winding, beautiful canyon. She has a very zen moment.

All of a sudden, Lily's head whips forward and she comes to a complete halt. A shiny white Mercedes just hit her bumper hard.

EXT. CANYON ROAD - CONTINUOUS

Lily steps out of her car. PETER (21) dressed funky as a backstreet boy wannabe, overly accessorized with bracelets and earrings. He's got great bone structure and is awkwardly tall with a 60s haircut. He runs up to her.

PETER: Are you okay? I wasn't paying attention. I'm so sorry, I was talking to my Mom, well actually she was screaming at me and she gets me so frustrated sometimes and I'm just really sorry.

Lily has an instant attraction but she's flustered a bit.

LILY: No it's okay. It was an accident. I'm just a little shaken up that's all.

PETER: I'll fix your bumper no problem. My cousin has a shop and will take care of it for you. Are you sure you're okay? I can take you to a hospital or call an ambulance if that makes you more comfortable.

LILY: No no I'm fine. I swear.

PETER: You don't have to worry about anything. My parents will pay for all of the trouble. I'm gonna text my cousin now and I'll get you towed to his shop. And if you decide you want to go to a doctor later, I'll pay for it.

LILY: Thanks. Okay um I'll take your number I guess. I was actually on my way to pick up keys to my new apartment and it's just a block away, so I can walk.

PETER: I can take you. I feel really bad.

LILY: No, I'll walk.

PETER: Ugh this sucks. Okay what's your number?

LILY: 8188675309

PETER: Got it. Just texted you. Can I walk with you? I just want to make sure you're really okay. Sometimes you can't feel it right away and I hit you kinda hard.

LILY: Okay. If you insist, but I really am okay.

INT. APARTMENT BUILDING HALLWAY - MOMENTS LATER

Peter and Lily walk down the narrow hallway each of them practically touching the side of each wall, leaving a small space between them. Lily is very short in comparison. Peter fixes each doormat that he walks past with his foot. Lily catches on after the third one he fixes and giggles.

LILY: I know. I hate that too.

PETER: I think I have mild OCD.

LILY: Oh I have it. I wish mine was like the cleaning kind, but it's mostly the counting kind.

PETER: What do you count?

Lily stops at apartment 101.

LILY: Um, lines on the road when I'm driving, trees, windows, pretty much anything.Well here we are. I just have to pick up my keys. You don't have to stay.

Lily KNOCKS on the door.

PETER: So do you want to grab a bite to eat?

NINA (35 pale, freckly with mop-like hair) the apartment manager whips her door open with too much energy. She has no sense of style and wears stirrup stretch pants with a long T-shirt that says Des Moines.

NINA: Hi you must be Lily? Aren't you a cute couple? Let me show you to your new apartment!

Lily and Peter look at each other and try not to laugh. They practically have to race down the hall to keep up with Nina. Peter holds Lily's hand.

PETER: I can't wait to see our new place.

Lily is amused.

NINA: Here it is! Welcome to your new home and welcome to the sierra ridge apartment family. You two will have to join us four our monthly barbecues. Of course you can barbecue anytime out by the pool, but the smell goes straight up to my window, so you have to invite me.

LILY: Peter actually loves to barbecue.

PETER: Yeah. All the time. We barbecue.

Nina hands them both a set of keys.

NINA: Oh my god, I forgot the chicken on the stove. My husband will kill me if I burn it. I'll talk to you guys later.

Nina takes off sprinting down the hallway.

PETER (flirts): Wow I've known you for 30 minutes and I already have a key.

LILY: Don't get too excited.

Lily takes the keys which are on a MICKEY AND MINNIE MOUSE HEART KEYCHAIN.

PETER: My cousin's assistant is gonna bring up all of your boxes in about 10 minutes and he said he can have your car done by tomorrow afternoon.

LILY: Oh wow. Thank you.

SAMANTHA (17) a 3 foot dwarf, comes zooming down the hallway at top speed on a scooter. She wears a fluorescent green helmet with matching elbow and knee pads. She heads straight toward Lily.

SAMANTHA: Move it or lose it!

Before Lily has a chance to move, Samantha plows over her toe.

LILY (Shocked): Ouch!

Peter tried to save her but it happened fast. Lily falls

into his arms. Samantha falls to the ground.

SAMANTHA: Thanks a lot bitch!

LILY: Excuse me?!

Samantha gets up and disappears around the corner.

PETER: That was bizarre.

LILY: Yeah, hang around me long enough and you'll get used to it. My mom says I'm cursed.

PETER: Are you okay?

LILY: Yeah it's just my toe. I'll live.

PETER: Can I take you to dinner?

LILY: I don't know.

PETER: Just this once so I can overcome my guilt and then you never have to see me again. I mean if you don't want to.

LILY: You don't have a girlfriend?

PETER: No. Do you have a boyfriend?

LILY: No.

PETER: Good. So is that a yes then?

LILY (smiles): Yeah. Okay.

INT. BATHROOM - EVENING

Lily is in her pink, floral bra as she finishes her makeup. The small orange radio with a broken handle is on the counter and 80s music plays. She concentrates as she puts on her lip liner.

Nina appears in her doorway.

LILY (screams): Oh my God!

Nina holds a brand new picnic basket.

NINA (laughs): It's just me. I brought you something.

LILY: How did you get in?

Nina shakes a big ring of master keys.

NINA: Perks of being the manager. I have keys to everyone's apartment. You're gonna love it here, it's like living in a dorm.

Lily realizes she's in her bra and grabs a towel to cover up.

LILY: Would you mind knocking next time? If I had my mace this could've ended badly.

NINA: I made you some baklava.

LILY: What's bakla... you know what, I'm running late for dinner with my fiance.

NINA: You don't want the baklava?

LILY (stern): Let's get something straight okay? You need to knock on my door next time and never let yourself in again.4

NINA: So if you're going out then I'll just bring it over for breakfast. My husband makes the best coffee, you're gonna love it.

Before Lily has a chance to answer, Nina dashes out.

INT. ELEVATOR - LATER

Peter wears black skinny jeans with a studded belt and a vintage t-shirt. Lily wears tight jeans and a pretty black top with stilettos. Her hair hangs over her small frame in curls.

Peter' cell phone RINGS.

PETER: Hi. Yes. Okay I will. Love you.

Peter puts his phone away.

PETER: Sorry that's so rude. It was just my mom reminding me for the tenth time to feed the dogs when I get back.

LILY: No need to apologize. My mom doesn't really check up on me. It's kind of cute.

EXT. PARKING STRUCTURE - MOMENTS LATER

Samantha frantically pushes the elevator button. She then picks up her scooter and slams it against the elevator wall.

INT. ELEVATOR - MOMENTS LATER

The elevator comes to a screeching halt.

LILY: Oh no, my biggest fear has always been to be stuck in one of these. I told you I'm cursed.

PETER: Relax, it's okay. I'm here.

Lily begins to hyperventilate and searches her purse

for her inhaler.

LILY: I'm claustrophobic and I have asthma.

Lily takes a hit off her inhaler and frantically pushes the first floor button.

PETER: Look here's a phone number. I'm gonna call for help.

LILY: Fuck. Why can't anything go right?

Lily hyperventilates again.

PETER: Hey it's okay. Just try to take a deep breath in. Let's sit down.

They sit on the floor. Lily puts her head between her knees. Peter rubs her back.

PETER: Breath in. That's it. It's been a crazy day and when we get out of here, I'm gonna help you forget about it. Okay.

The elevator makes a jerking motion. Lily puts her head in his chest and Peter holds her.

LILY: Oh my god. It's gonna collapse.

Lily grabs onto Peter afraid.

PETER: Okay, let's think about this. Even if it falls, we're probably like two feet away from the ground.

Suddenly the elevator door opens to the parking structure. An angry Samantha storms into the elevator. Lily is slightly embarrassed and pulls away from Peter.

SAMANTHA: Are you done fucking around yet? Some of us actually use this as a way to get home.

LILY: Oh it's you again! For your information we were stuck.

SAMANTHA: Please spare me the details.

The elevator door closes on Samantha flipping them off.

INT. THE TRIG NIGHTCLUB - LATER

Peter and Lily sit face-to-face, criss-cross in a swinging chair held by cables from the ceiling. They sip cocktails and swing like children. It's dimly lit by blue neon lights. The room is small with lots of mirrors and eccentric lounge spaces. The FUNKY DJ spins underground hip hop.

LILY: That was the best creme brulee I've had in my whole life.

PETER: I know right. My mom loves it too.

LILY: No offense, but you're kind of a mama's boy aren't you?

PETER: No, not at all.

LILY: Yes, you definitely are.

PETER: You've never met my mom. She's insane.

LILY: I can prove it. Check your cell phone.

Peter amuses her and unlocks his phone.

LILY: Any messages? I bet there are at least three.

PETER: You're absolutely wrong. There's only two.

They share a LAUGH.

LILY (teases): There's nothing wrong with that. It's just that every Cosmo I've ever read says to steer clear of guys like you.

PETER: I feel like you might kind of like me in spite of my many flaws.

LILY: Maybe just a little.

Peter and Lily lean in for their first sweet kiss.

PETER: What about you? Are you daddy's little girl?

LILY: Uh no.

PETER: You know, you're really beautiful. I've been trying to think of a way to say it without sounding lame cause I'm sure you hear it all the time.

LILY: Only from men in pickup trucks driving by. And thanks. You're beautiful too. I also have flaws. I know it sounds crazy but I think I'm cursed.

PETER: You're not joking about that?

LILY: I don't know. My mom told me that my grand-mother was a witch in Italy and lived in Benevento where all of the Italian witches are from and anyway she says she put a curse on me.

PETER: Whoa that's so interesting. I mean not the

curse part. So are you a witch.

LILY: No! I mean maybe by blood and if it were the 1800s I guess I may have been burned at the stake but I don't like practice witchcraft.

PETER: So why do you think you're cursed?

NINA: You've known me for a short time. Can't you already see it?

PETER: I mean I know we were in an accident, but if that didn't happen maybe we would've never met.

NINA: That's true.

PETER: Maybe just maybe, if you look at everything from a different perspective, you can laugh at the dwarf who hates you for no reason and all of the other chaos.

NINA: I mean I do have great stories for days.

PETER: See? Cursed or not, I'm really looking forward to getting to know you.

NINA: Mama's boy or not, same.

INT. LILY'S APARTMENT - MORNING

Lily does yoga on a bright blue mat. Soothing MUSIC plays. She wears flannel pajama bottoms and a sports bra. Someone BANGS on her door. Lily is startled and pauses the music.

LILY: Who is it?

NINA (O.S.): Good morning!! It's nina!

LILY: I just woke up, can you come back in 15 minutes.

NINA (O.S.): I've been knocking all morning. You have a delivery.

LILY (annoyed): It's probably a mistake.

NINA (O.S.): No it isn't!

Lily grudgingly puts on her glasses and opens the door. Nina stands cheerfully with a pot of coffee and the baklava.

NINA: I knew that would get you to open the door.

LILY: So there isn't a package?

NINA: No yeah there's a package, but I'm not gonna let you have it until you have some breakfast with me.

LILY (irritated): Okay sure.

Nina walks straight to the kitchen and opens random cupboards.

NINA: Where are your coffee mugs?

LILY: Top left.

Nina grabs 2 handmade ceramic mugs. And pours coffee. She prepares the table with the intensity of a little girl playing tea party. She folds two paper napkins into swans.

NINA: Come sit down. Here taste this!

Nina hands Lily a piece of baklava and a cup of coffee. Lily takes a bite and is almost mad at how good it tastes.

LILY: It's really good. Um what were you saying about a package?

NINA: Oh you're no fun. Fine I'll go get it.

Nina runs out and comes back in with a huge refrigerator sized box on a dolly.

NINA: I don't know what's in here, but I can't wait to find out. Come on, let's open it!

LILY: I'm gonna open it later. I have an audition and need to shower and get ready.

NINA: Oh wow. I didn't know you were an actress. Can I come? For moral support?

LILY: No that's not allowed but thanks for everything.

NINA: Alright, I can take a hint. I'll grab my coffee pot later.

Nina runs off.

LILY (under her breath): No you cannot take a hint.

Lily is confused and begins to open the box. Inside she finds towels, a mid-century-modern chair with a blue faux fur cushion, a beautiful fake house plant, coffee maker/frother, lots of toiletries, a throw rug and a cosmo magazine. On the cover the words "Why

Mama's Boys Make Sensitive and Caring Boyfriends."
Lily makes a call.

LILY: Mom?

A CLICK and DIAL TONE. Lily makes another call.

LILY: Peter?

PETER: Good morning!

LILY: Did you...

PETER: I did. I wanted to send you a care package because I still feel incredibly guilty about hitting your
car. I hope it wasn't too forward of me.

LILY: I don't know what to say. You really didn't have
to do that.

PETER: Okay good so you're not mad?

LILY: You just showered me with gifts, why would I
be mad?

PETER: You're a doll.

EXT. SIDEWALK - AFTERNOON

Lily is in a rush with a script in her hand. A bird
poops on her head. Lily screams.

LILY: Oh my god, no!

Lily touches it and gets it on her hand. She digs
through her purse and still walks. She pulls out some
kleenex and tries to get it out.

INT. CASTING DIRECTOR'S OFFICE - AFTERNOON

Lily stands in the middle of the room in a fluffy white robe. You can see some bird poop streaked on the side of her hair. A table of exec types sit at a table in front of her with arms crossed. Lily is extremely nervous and clenches the script. The CASTING DIRECTOR (30) stands directly behind the camera directly in front of her.

CASTING DIRECTOR: And Action.

Lily sets down the script on a chair, takes a candle and matches out of her bag and proceeds to light a candle on a small table. She then picks up the script and lays down on the floor next to the candle as if she were in a bathtub. Execs look confused.

LILY: Thanks for drawing my bath. It was such a long and treacherous day. Now leave me alone with my thoughts.

Lily swooshes her hand and hits the script off the table and onto the candle. It catches fire and she doesn't notice at first.

EXEC #1: I told you we should've stopped her. Who brings props to an audition anyway!

Lily now sees the FIRE, stands up and fans the paper with her robe which only makes the flame larger.

LILY: I'm so sorry.

Lily throws the flaming script into the metal trash can. Temporary relief and then we see a can of hairspray underneath the script and a mini explosion.

CASTING DIRECTOR (panicking): Everybody out!

Lily grabs her purse and is the first one out the door. She hits one of the execs with her bag on her way out by mistake.

EXT. MIMMO AND MICHELA'S HOUSE - DAY

Vinnie mows the lawn as his older GIRLFRIEND (24) lays in a lawn chair on her stomach with her string bikini top totally untied. Vinnie leaves the lawn-mower running and runs over to Lily.

VINNIE: You better leave. Ma's in a bad mood.

LILY: I need to grab my retainer. Vinnie, why is there a naked girl in the front yard?

VINNIE: She's hot isn't she?

LILY: How old is she?

VINNIE: Nevermind that. Go get your retainer before you turn back into gap-tooth-gail.

LILY: You're so stupid. What kind of girl lays out naked at your parent's house? She looks like she could be your zia.

VINNIE: Mom's fine with it. She even made her breakfast.

LILY: She spent the night?

Vinnie smirks and Lily is visually disgusted. Lily attempts to open the front door which is locked. She

RINGS the doorbell and Michela answers.

MICHELA: What do you want? You need money, here.

She takes money out of her apron and hands it to Lily.

LILY: No Ma, I don't want money. I just forgot my retainer and wanted to visit with you.

MICHELA: I don't want to talk.

Lily points to the girl in the lawnchair.

LILY: Ma, did you see that?

MICHELA: What? She's a nice girl. She helped me make bread this morning. Why should you care anyway? You don't want to live here anymore.

LILY: Why do you let Vinnie have a girl spend the night? You never let me do that?

MICHELA: He's a boy.

LILY: So what?

MICHELA: He can zip us his pants and say goodbye. You, you can get pregnant and then no one will want you.

LILY: Mom that is so old fashioned. That's not the way it is.

MICHELA: You should be thankful that I didn't let that happen to you like it happened to me.

LILY: So that's it, that's why you hate me? I'm the big mistake right?

MICHELA: I didn't say that, you said it.

LILY: Alright, bye Ma. Bye Vinnie.

VINNIE: Hey Lily, can me and Joey come over sometime?

LILY: Yeah whenever you want.

They are a family that fights but stays together. Lily fights back her tears.

INT. AGENT'S OFFICE - LATER

VIRGINIA (75) is dressed in a Hawaiian print moo moo. Her blue-black hair is up in a beehive and she is smoking weed out of a hookah. Dark cherrywood furniture lines her office walls. Pictures of Marilyn Monroe and old movie stars align the walls. Her desk is a cluttered mess and overflows with headshots.

VIRGINIA (New Jersey Accent): Lily, my love, what happened?

LILY: I thought it would be memorable to use props in the scene. It was an accident.

VIRGINIA: Here take a hit? You're always so anxious. It will calm you down honey.

LILY: No thanks, I'm allergic.

VIRGINIA: You really need to learn how to relax. You should start meditating. Or how about some xanax, I have some extras around here somewhere.

Virginia digs through her messy office drawers.

LILY: That's okay, I'm already messed up enough as it is.

VIRGINIA: Are you insinuating that I am messed up because I smoke weed, which is legal and beneficial and take xanax which is a prescription by a medical doctor?

LILY: No not at all. I'm so sorry. It came out wrong.

VIRGINIA: You've almost cost me my reputation, you know that?

LILY: I'm sorry, I don't know what to say.

VIRGINIA: Look honey, when you get your act together come and see me. This just isn't working out.

LILY: Please give me another chance.

VIRGINIA: You're not worth the risk honey. Who brings props to a callback.

LILY: Okay. Well I'm going to make it with or without you. But I respect your decision.

Virginia takes a long hit out of her hookah pipe.

VIRGINIA: That's what they all say sweetie. Good luck.

EXT. LUNA CAFE - MORNING

Lily and Nina sit at an outdoor table surrounded

by potted plants and sip coffee. A handsome waiter drops off a couple salads.

NINA: I just love Evan to death, but sometimes he goes too far.

LILY: What do you mean?

NINA: Well he says that since I'm older and got to live my life that he should be able to experiment while he's still young.

LILY (uninterested): Really?

NINA: Yeah so he asks me if I'll have a threesome with him.

Lily takes a big bite of her salad to avoid having to talk.

NINA: So I don't know, what do you think?

BRANDON (refined, handsome 21) walks up to their table with BRANDY (18 head to toe in fashion, looks high on something).

BRANDON: Well well well, who do we have here?

LILY: What do you want?

BRANDON: Lily, you're always such a charmer aren't you?

Brandy starts playing with his ear and grabbing him impatiently.

LILY: I'm still waiting for my last check.

BRANDON: Oh you didn't receive that. I'm so sorry.

LILY: Whatever it was just for one shift.

Brandon opens his wallet and pulls out two hundred dollars and lays it on the table.

BRANDON: That should cover your hourly and tips. If you ever need a job you're always welcome back. Do me a favor and tell your brother Vinnie I'm so sorry I haven't had a chance to call him back yet and I paid you.

Lily puts the cash in her purse.

LILY: Yep.

BRANDY: I'm hungry babe.

BRANDON: Okay baby, let's go. Bye Lily. So nice to see you.

Lily rolls her eyes. The couple walk away.

NINA: What was that about?

LILY: Ugh he owns La Porque and he hit on me so I walked out mid-shift. He's so gross.

Nina puts her hand on her heart dramatically.

NINA: I'm so sorry girl.

A silent moment.

NINA: So what do you say we have a threesome?

Lily can't hide her annoyance anymore.

LILY: What? No. If any guy ever asked me that I'd tell him to go to hell.

NINA: Well we're a liberal household.

LILY: To each their own.

Samantha the neighbor walks by them with her father ROCKO (40 long sideburns disheveled, also a little person). Samantha is in tears and her father holds her by the back of the arm. Lily looks briefly then continues to eat her salad. Awkward all around. Lily looks at her buzzing phone. She reads a text message from Peter.

PETER (text): HEY ARE YOU BUSY? WANT TO GO ON A LITTLE ADVENTURE WITH ME RN?

LILY (text): YES PLEASE SAVE ME. I'M AT LUNCH WITH NINA.

PETER (text):   OKAY I'LL PICK YOU UP IN 20 MINUTES IF THAT WORKS.

LILY (text): Yay!!!

INT. PETER' CONVERTIBLE MERCEDES - DAY

Peter and Lily are dressed in big sweaters and scarves as they cruise down PCH. Lily's hair is a crazy curly mess and keeps blowing in her face.

PETER: Okay, so are you ready for the surprise?

LILY: Yes!

PETER: Have you ever been to a movie at Hollywood

Forever Cemetery?

LILY: They have movies at a cemetery?

PETER: I know it sounds kind of morbid, but it's actually really fun and tonight they are doing the Hitchcock movie birds. I thought we could stop by a market to grab a few things..

LILY: Okay but I'm sort of terrified of crows. They're too smart. Once I saved a baby bird from a crow and I swear to god, I woke up to my car covered in bird shit. And it had to be on purpose.

PETER: Well you did probably ruin their meal for the night.

Peter laughs while his phone RINGS through the bluetooth. He ignores it.

LILY: Is that your mom?

PETER: Yeah but I'll call her later.

The phone RINGS again.

LILY: You can answer it. I'll be quiet.

PETER: Nah it's fine.

The phone RINGS nonstop.

PETER: Okay, maybe I should see what's up. Hi mom!

SOPHIA (O.S. Crying): Peter! Nana is in the hospital.

She is crying so hard, he can barely understand.

PETER: Mom, mom it's gonna be okay. Where are you

and what happened?

SOPHIA (O.S.)L: I'm at Oak Glen Hospital. She fell down on the terrace. Please come as soon as you can.

PETER: Don't worry I'm about 15 minutes away actually. See you soon. Love you.

SOPHIA (O.S.): Love you honey.

LILY: Oh my god. I'm so sorry. Fuck I told you I'm cursed.

PETER: What? No. This has nothing to do with you. She's 98. I know this is weird timing but would you mind coming with me?

LILY: I mean I can just uber home from the hospital.

PETER: It's totally up to you. Whatever makes you more comfortable.

LILY: Yeah I'm sure this is a tough time for your family. I'll just get an uber.

Peter and Lily pull up to the Oak Glen Hospital. Peter parks next to a Black Range Rover. Peter' Mom SOPHIA (stylish in a pageant way, lots of gold jewelry and perfect makeup) cries in the passenger side. Peter hurries out of the car.

EXT. HOSPITAL PARKING LOT - CONTINUOUS

Lily is a bit uncomfortable and not sure if she should get out of the car or wait.

Peter turns to Lily and silently nods his apology to

Lily then comforts his mom.

Lily opens the car door as quietly as she can while Sophia steps out of her car. Sophia spots Lily.

SOPHIA: Come here doll. I'm so sorry to interrupt your night.

Lily stops like a frightened cat.

LILY: No, it's totally fine. I'm really sorry and hope she's okay.

Sophia motions for Lily to come closer. Sophia grasps Lily in a big hug while crying.

SOPHIA (to Peter): I'm sorry I'm never nice to your friend's Peter. Life is too short.

PETER: No it's okay Mom.

SOPHIA: What's your name doll?

LILY: I'm Lily.

SOPHIA: So nice to finally meet you.

LILY: Oh no, we just...

Lily is not sure what to do in the awkward embrace and stops mid-sentence. Peter puts a hand on each of their shoulders.

PETER: Mom let's go inside.

Sophia snaps out of the crying and hug.

SOPHIA: Okay.

Sophia grabs Lily and Peter's hand and they walk into the hospital. Peter and Lily exchange a look that makes them both feel more comfortable with the situation.

INT. HOSPITAL ROOM - MOMENTS LATER

Lily stands in the doorway while Sophia and Peter join Peter's Dad (HENRY - he's much older than Sophia and well put together) standing around the Grandmother CATHERINE's hospital bed. She's a pretty old woman with long white hair.

Sophia hugs Henry and then looks up at Lily with a smile.

SOPHIA: Come dear. Henry, this is Lily.

Lily walks over and Henry reaches out for a hug.

LILY: Oh hi, Mr. Schaffer.

HENRY: Hi Lily it's nice to meet you.

LILY: You too. I'm sorry about everything.

HENRY: Don't be silly. You all got here just in time, she just came out of hip surgery.

Peter is holding his grandmother's hand and Lily stands next to him. Suddenly one of Catherine's eyes pops open as if the other one is stuck shut.

CATHERINE: Well, I'm still alive!

Everyone sighs relief and LAUGHTER erupts.

SOPHIA: Oh mom, you stubborn woman.

Sophia kisses her mother and everyone is relieved.

CATHERINE: Who is this pretty girl?

Catherine squints to see her better.

PETER: This is Lily, Grandma. We were on our way to a movie when I found out so we came here right away.

CATHERINE: I'm sorry I ruined your date.

LILY & PETER: No, not at all.

Catherine is a bit senile, but still very witty.

CATHERINE: I had to almost die for you to bring a girl around.

PETER: Grandma...

HENRY: How do you feel lovey?

Catherine ignores and fixates on Lily.

CATHERINE: So what do you do Lily?

LILY (embarrassed): Oh, I'm an actress and I work at a restaurant.

CATHERINE: Lovely. And what does your Dad do?

LILY: Um, he works at the docks.

CATHERINE: Is he a sailor?

LILY: No, he's a fisherman. My family owns a small fish market in Malibu.

CATHERINE (to Peter): She's a looker and we have money. I think it's a perfect match. Where is your family from?

PETER: Nana, you must be tired.

LILY: Oh it's fine. I'm a first generation Italian.

Catherine smiles big.

CATHERINE: Wonderful. Peter is half Italian from my side. The good side. The other half is Irish.

Sophia winks at Lily. Henry and Peter are uncomfortable with Catherine's interrogation. Lily smiles and tries to be a good sport.

CATHERINE: Does your family have properties or a trust?

HENRY & SOPHIA: Mom!

CATHERINE: You're lovely darling.

HENRY: Oh lovey, you're loopy from the pain meds. Why don't you close your eyes and get some sleep.

A NURSE (extremely old and grumpy) enters.

NURSE: Alright, it's time for medicine.

CATHERINE: If the surgery didn't kill me. This wicked witch might.

Catherine obliges and takes a pill with some oj.

INT. PETER' CONVERTIBLE MERCEDES - LATER

Some old school hip hop plays on the radio.

PETER: I hope you're not terrified. That's not at all how I planned this night to go and I'm really sorry my nana was so forward.

LILY: No, it's not your fault. I can't wait until I'm eighty and can get away with saying whatever I want. I'm just glad she's okay.

PETER: Me too. Not to scare you even more, but my family doesn't usually warm up to my friends so easily so that was actually an example of things going well.

LILY: They seem really nice. I should probably go and I'm sure you have to get up early for work.

Peter puts his hand on Lily's at a stop light with the beautiful coast in the background. They lean in for a sweet kiss.

PETER: It's kind of embarrassing, but I don't have a job right now. But please don't think I'm a spoiled trust fund brat, I mean I am that...

LILY: I won't judge you if you don't judge me. My parents have money, but they don't spend it. My dad has been driving that same car since I was a baby and there's no way they will help me. Since I left home before marriage, I'm basically cut off.

PETER: I'm really sorry. If it makes you feel any better, if my music doesn't take off soon and I don't do what they want me to do, I'm totally gonna get cut off.

LILY: I doubt your mom would let that happen. My parents on the other hand are old school. Me and my cousins learned how to swim by being thrown in the pool.

Peter brings Lily's hand up to his lips at a stop light. Their chemistry is electric.

PETER: That's tragic I'm sorry. Well it's been 24 hours but I feel like I've known you my whole life.

LILY: It is weird. I feel really comfortable.

They kiss a little too long and the car behind HONKS at them.

PETER: Well I can't wait to see you again.

LILY: I'm here right now though.

They kiss again even more passionately.

INT. LILY'S KITCHEN - DAY

Lily sits atop the ugly formica countertop and carefully lays down marble white contact paper. She proudly finishes the last corner and pulls the blinds up.

The blinds fall down on top of her. She peeks her head up in between two blinds as the front door knob begins to turn.

Nina walks in with her huge key ring.

NINA: Oh my god!

LILY: Please just knock...

Nina sprints to Lily and begins to untangle her from the blinds.

LILY: I'm fine. I really need my privacy.

NINA: Don't be silly, I heard that loud noise on my way to get the mail. You poor thing. Oh shit your eye!

Nina runs to the freezer and grabs a bag of peas. Lily gets off the countertop. Nina puts the bag of peas on her eye.

NINA: You're gonna wanna keep that iced. That's gonna be a shiner.

LILY: Great I don't have health insurance as of last week. Ouch.

NINA: Not to worry. I have an eye patch from my eye ulcer and you can borrow it.

Lily wants to resist, but gives in.

LILY: Okay, thanks Nina.

Nina is pleased. She hugs Lily.

NINA: We're gonna be best friends. BRB bitch.

Lily gets a text from Peter. HEY LILY. WANT TO JOIN MY FAMILY FOR DINNER TONIGHT? Lily smiles.

INT. PETER'S HOUSE - NIGHT

The dining room is enormous and decorated with pin-striped wallpaper and fresh flowers. The table is made of actual white marble adorned with fine China and far too many kinds of silverware. Peter and Lily sit across from each other, Lily sports a black eye patch. A gigantic window overlooks the ocean.

Peter's mother Sophia wears all white linen and her hair is pinned tightly up. Henry is in a sweater vest and nana Catherine sits in a wheelchair with a flashy red blouse. Peter and Lily look extra casual in comparison. They eat in silence. The sun beautifully sets over the ocean. Lily SNEEZES aggressively into her elbow.

EVERYONE: God bless you.

LILY: Thanks, I always sneeze when I look at the sun.

SOPHIA: Maybe we should switch seats dear.

LILY: No thank you. I'll be okay.

Sophia gets up and shuts the curtains completely and the room darkens. Sun peeks through the side and aims directly at the one eye without the patch. Lily is about to sneeze again, but loses it. Everyone pretends not to notice.

CATHERINE (to Lily): You're so pretty. Eat your carrots. It's good for the eyes and you don't want to lose the other one.

LILY: Oh I didn't lose it. It's just a bit swollen because I hit my head earlier.

SOPHIA: Mother please.

Henry clears his throat. Peter gives Lily a comforting smile.

HENRY: Does your family belong to the tennis club?

LILY: Oh no. My dad spends most of his free time fishing and working on his cars.

SOPHIA: Doesn't he have people who do that?

LILY: He does but he loves being on the ocean before the market opens every day and he's been working on a really old Rolls Royce since I was five.

SOPHIA: Fascinating. We go to Italy once a year and it's beautiful. Is your family Northern or gypsy? I'm sorry, I mean Roma. Is that the proper term?

PETER: Mom?

SOPHIA: What? She looks very much like the Gypsies eh hem Roma in Capri. Henry?

HENRY: No not at all.

LILY: No. My mom actually has stories that the gypsies stole her chickens and gold when she was little.

LAUGHTER breaks the tension. Sophia gets up and walks over to Lily.

SOPHIA: Here darling you're using the wrong fork.

Remember you start at the fork closest to your plate.

LILY: Okay thanks.

PETER: Mom, that wasn't necessary.

SOPHIA: I'm just trying to help her, maybe no one ever showed her the right way.

Lily smiles and holds back her annoyance. Catherine is oblivious to everyone and scoops some mashed potatoes into her cloth napkin, carefully folds it and tucks it up her sleeve.

HENRY: So Lily, are you in school?

LILY: I'm actually transferring to a university in the fall.

HENRY: Oh great. What university?

LILY: Either Pepperdine or USC, I got accepted to both and haven't decided yet.

Henry is impressed. Sophia is annoyed.

HENRY: And what will you study?

LILY: Film if I go to USC and Law if I go to Pepperdine.

HENRY: Why not entertainment law. More stable than a career in film, but still in an industry you enjoy.

LILY: I've never really thought about that, but thanks for the idea.

HENRY: Maybe you can talk our Peter into going

back.

PETER: Let's not discuss that now please.

SOPHIA: What is a piece of paper going to do? Our grandchildren's children are set for life.

PETER: I already told you I'm passionate about my music now and I can go to college any time in the future.

CATHERINE (to Lily): Are your boobs real? You know I was a DD at one time. And mine were real.

Lily and Peter try not to laugh.

SOPHIA: Mother I think it's time to take your medication.

CATHERINE: Oh who needs it, I'm gonna go one way or another. I want to talk to Lily. She's the interesting one.

SOPHIA: Alright Mom, please take your pills now.

CATHERINE (to Lily): It's a terrible thing to get old. They treat you like a child. Lily. You must be named after the flower.

Lily looks at her phone.

LILY: Oh I'm so sorry, I didn't realize how late it is and I work tonight.

SOPHIA: Where do you work?

LILY: I'm a server.

SOPHIA: At your family fish market?

LILY: Oh no, I worked there a long time when I was younger. I work at Leno's.

HENRY: See that Peter, you should get a job.

PETER: I'm gonna walk Lily out.

A maid comes to clear the plates. Peter moves Lily's chair out.

INT. LENO'S RESTAURANT - EVENING

Lily wears her eye patch and a silly frilly server shirt and punches in an order at the computer. CLAY (25) really muscular and unattractive, piped up on steroids comes up to Lily in a frenzy.

CLAY: Oh shit, it's you. Are you almost done? I just got double seated.

LILY: It's going to be a minute, I'm ringing in the order for my big party.

Lily continues.

CLAY: I need to do something really quick.

LILY: Okay, well station 2 is probably open.

CLAY: Come on. You always take for freaking ever.

LILY: Well I'd go a lot faster if you'd stop talking to me.

CLAY: You're such a bitch.

Clay walks away pissed off and can be seen talking to CHRISTINA (37) the general manager of Leno's. They both walk over to Lily.

CHRISTINA (bitchy): Lily is there a problem?

LILY: No, not at all. I'm almost done.

CHRISTINA: Come on Lily, what's going on? You have a weird eye patch and now this?

LILY: I'm just trying to finish my order.

Lily makes a final adjustment and sends the order.

LILY (to Clay): There, I'm done. All yours.

CHRISTINA: I don't like your attitude. Meet me in my office.

LILY: But I have tables.

CHRISTINA: Clay will take over. Meet me in my office.

LILY: I'm more than happy to, but can I please finish up my tables? I just got a 13 top and I really need the money.

CHRISTINA: This is insubordination.

LILY: No it isn't. I literally have done nothing wrong and I'm trying to work.

CHRISTINA: Give me your card.

Lily hands her the card.

CHRISTINA: You can leave your apron upstairs. You're fired!

LILY: What? I'm fired for what?

CHRISTINA: Insubordination!

Clay loves it.

LILY: This is ridiculous. You can't fire me.

CHRISTINA: I can and I did.

LILY: Fine! But don't think I won't tell corporate about you and Clay fucking around in the walk in.

A female customer KAREN (62) overhears the argument in disgust.

KAREN: Such awful language. I thought this was a family restaurant.

Christina turns around to comfort the customer.

CHRISTINA: I'm sorry. You're right and she's leaving.

Lily is stunned. She takes off her apron and throws it on the counter.

LILY: I'm outta here.

Lily flips them off with both hands and leaves.

INT. APARTMENT BUILDING HALLWAY - LATER

Lily walks toward her apartment upset. Samantha cries next to her front door in the hallway. Lily wipes her own tears and walks into her apartment.

INT. APARTMENT - MOMENTS LATER

Lily throws down her purse and keys and sits with her back leaning on the front door. She lets the tears flow. She dries her eyes, gets up and opens her door, peeks her head out.

INT. APARTMENT BUILDING HALLWAY - CONTINUOUS

Samantha still cries. They look at each other like deers in headlights.

LILY: Hey are you okay?

SAMANTHA: Fuck off!

LILY: You're one angry girl.

SAMANTHA: Oh yeah, like you have any room to be so judgmental elevator slut!

LILY: I'm going to ignore that because much worse has happened today. I just wanted to make sure you're not dying or anything.

SAMANTHA: Yep. I'm not dying.

LILY: Okay great. Forget I asked.

Lily slams the door shut. Then she looks out the peephole and feels bad.

INT. BATHROOM - LATER

Lily wears pjs and sits on the toilet. She has earbuds on.

LILY: Your family isn't perfect but neither is mine. You have no idea.

PETER: They made you so they can't be so bad. I think you're a sweetheart.

LILY: I've had a rough day. But my whole life is like this. I'm warning you.

Lily mutes the phone and flushes. Suddenly the toilet overflows. She unmutes by mistake.

LILY: Oh my god!

PETER: What's going on?

LILY: Oh god this is just what I need today. My toilet is overflowing.

PETER: How cute. You were peeing on the phone with me.

LILY: You caught me. Pretty sexy hu?

The toilet uncontrollably overflows everywhere.

PETER: You wanna call your manager and call me right back.

LILY: Ok. Bye.

Lily dials.

LILY: Nina? Hi it's Lily. My toilet is overflowing.

Lily tiptoes out of the soggy bathroom.

INT. LIVING ROOM - MOMENTS LATER

Water slowly seeps out of the bathroom and Lily puts down a towel to block it while balancing a phone on her ear.

NINA (O.S.): Figures. The plumbing in this building sucks. I'll send someone out Monday morning.

LILY: Okay thanks. Wait, today is Saturday.

Lily begins to pace.

NINA (O.S.): Yep. It's the weekend. Our plumber works Monday and Thursday.

LILY: Well can't you get someone else?

NINA (O.S.): Oh I could never. He would be so offended if he knew I hired someone else. Op, gotta go, the man is home. If you need to use the restroom, you're free to use ours. Bye hun!

Lily throws her phone onto the futon. It misses and hits the floor. The glass shatters. Lily is unbothered.

LILY (to herself): If? No maybe I'll hold it til Monday you stupid bitch!

The phone RINGS. Lily grabs it and nicks her finger on the broken screen. It bleeds.

LILY: Hello.

She sucks on the small cut to make it stop bleeding. Plops down into her beanbag.

PETER (O.S.): You good?

LILY: They're coming on Monday.

PETER: What? They can't leave you like that.

LILY: I know.

PETER: Okay. Just pack some stuff and you can stay here with me at my parent's house for the weekend.

LILY: I don't know. I think I'd feel weird.

PETER: It's fine. Trust me. Besides, you can't stay there without functioning plumbing.

LILY: If you're sure it's okay.

PETER: I'm sure. Plus I'd love to spend the weekend with you.

LILY: Well I have plenty of free time cause I just got fired tonight.

PETER: You're just having some bad luck. Don't worry okay. I'll see you soon.

Lily lets out a big sigh of frustration.

INT. PETER'S FAMILY ROOM - LATER

The room is cozy with plaid couches, two lounge chairs and a plush red carpet. A big screen TV is at the end with a large selection of dvd's. Peter plugs in a fancy foot bath for Lily and massages her feet as they watch HEATHERS.

LILY: Where is everyone?

PETER: They went to the show.

Lily begins to enjoy the pampering.

LILY: This is not a bad ending to this horrific day.

PETER: And you deserve it.

LILY: I don't know where you came from.

PETER: That was the best car accident ever.

LILY: Serendipitous

PETER: I feel so lucky meeting you. I know you're going through some stuff, but you're really strong and I got your back.

LILY: No one has ever said that to me before.

PETER: I'm going to make you a sandwich and we can cuddle and watch movies all night until you forget about everything. We get to be together all weekend.

Lily combs her fingers through his hair. They both lean into a passionate kiss.

MONTAGE:

Slow motion of passionate kisses.

They sit opposite sides of the couch and try to catch popcorn with their mouths.

Both of them are asleep with their clothes still on, wrapped in each other's arms.

Lily's cell phone RINGS.

EXT. LILY'S APARTMENT BUILDING - DAY

Vinnie and Joey BUZZ Lily's apartment.

VINNIE: Are you sure this is the right one moron?

JOEY: How am I supposed to know I've never been here. Call her cell phone.

Vinnie pulls out a flip phone from his leather jacket and DIALS. Joey touches Vinnie's hair.

JOEY: What did you put in your hair? You greasy fuck.

Vinnie slaps his hand away.

VINNIE: Yeah Lily, it's Vinnie. You told us to come over and we're here. Where are you? Nevermind... Alright fine, meet us at the deli, but hurry cause you know how ma gets.

JOEY: Tell her to hurry up.

VINNIE (to Joey): I did, what's the matter with you.

Vinnie pushes Joey who starts to fall to the ground but snaps up and walks away strutting.

EXT. TABLE AT THE DELI - DAY

Lily and her family are seated around a plastic table on a plant filled patio. Everyone, except Lily, chain smokes. Vinnie dumps salt on the table so he can balance the shaker. Michela picks up some salt and throws it over her shoulder.

MIMMO: Where were you? You said to come over and then you wasn't there.

LILY: I had to stay at a friend's house cause my toilet overflowed.

Vinnie and Joey LAUGH.

MIMMO: Don't you own a plunger? You gotta have a plunger when you wanna be an adult.

LILY: Yes Dad, but it was a big mess.

MIMMO: What big mess? All you had to do was plunge it. I would've done it, but I couldn't. You know I'm doing the bricks in the yard for your mother.

MICHELA: Yeah. It looks so good. Like Italy.

Vinnie and Joey nudge each other.

VINNIE: Hey Lily, what's that on your neck?

JOEY: Maybe it was a leech!

LILY: What are you talking about?

Everyone focuses on the bright blue HICKEY on Lily's neck.

MICHELA: Did you get hurt?

JOEY: So where did you stay last night?

LILY: I told you a friend.

VINNIE: So what was the lucky bastard's name?

LILY: Vinnie shut up you're so gross.

MIMMO: What this. You stayed at a boy's house?

Lily is saved by the red head, freckly WAITER (18).

WAITER: Hi. How are you today? Our specials..

MIMMO: I'm not doing too good.

They all stare at him. He's frazzled.

WAITER (intimidated): I'm sorry. Welcome to the deli. We have two specials today. The first is a...

MIMMO: I'll take a bacon sandwich with a lot of mayo.

MICHELA: What mayonnaise? You have high cholesterol!

MIMMO: I said a lot of mayo. She doesn't know what she's talking about.

The waiter puts his nose in his pad afraid to make eye contact.

MICHELA: Fine, don't listen to me, you never do anyway.

LILY: I'll have a caesar salad with no croutons and a cup of french onion soup. But do me a favor, I worked at a restaurant, can you make sure the bowl is really clean without any leftover gunks of cheese on it from the last person?

The waiter pushes up his glasses and writes intently.

WAITER: Oh yeah for sure. I'll tell the chef.

JOEY: Excuse my family's bad restaurant manners. He's gonna spit in our food you idiots.

WAITER: Oh I wouldn't...

JOEY: I'll take a steak sandwich just the way it comes.

WAITER: How would you like that prepared sir?

JOEY: How would I like it prepared? I told you. Just cooked. Thank you.

Joey whispers to Vinnie while trying to make a good face to the waiter.

JOEY (to Vinnie): This guy's a real dummy.

WAITER: Got it.

MICHELA: I don't want anything.

The waiter looks at Lily.

MICHELA: Maybe some soup.

WAITER: We have beef barley and cream of spinach.

MICHELA: Spinach.

WAITER: Would you like a cup or a bowl?

MICHELA: Yes I'll have the tea in the cup and the soup in the bowl.

Another CUSTOMER (46) at a table ten feet away waves her hand at the waiter. Waiter grits his teeth into a fake smile totally flustered.

VINNIE: I'll take a cheeseburger and fries. But make sure there's no pink in the burger cause we will sue the shit out of you if I get sick you understand?

Joey gathers all the menus and hands them to the waiter and smiles. The waiter takes them and walks away.

JOEY: What's the matter with yous. He's gonna fuck with our food I know it.

Michela begins to wrap up the salt and pepper shakers in her napkin, she looks around and slips it in her big black purse.

LILY: Ma what are you doing? You can't do that!

MICHELA: Nothing, shut up and mind your own business.

LILY: Ma take those out of your purse!

MIMMO: Leave her alone, everybody does that goody two shoes.

LILY: What is the matter with you? You have fifty salt and pepper shakers at home.

VINNIE (laughing): How do you think she got so many.

JOEY: It's a collection.

LILY: Ma take them out or I'm leaving.

MICHELA: Well now I can't he's coming.

LILY: Give me your purse!

VINNIE: Lily, your honesty gives me goosebumps.

LILY: You shut up!

MIMMO: That's enough!

Michela hands over the purse. Lily unwraps the shakers. The waiter walks toward the table.

JOEY (whispers): Here he comes, put them back.

Lily shoves them back in the purse.

WAITER: Excuse me, but may I ask what you're doing with the deli's salt and pepper shakers?

LILY: Um nothing, I was just...

WAITER (calmly): I'm gonna have to ask for those back.

MIMMO: I'm sorry she has sticky fingers you know. It's a sickness.

Mimmo does the crazy sign with his hand.

WAITER: Please leave the shakers on the table and I'm going to have to ask you to leave.

They all get up like routine and climb over the patio chain instead of going out the front door. Michela has some trouble so Mimmo helps her over.

INT. LILY'S APARTMENT - LATER

The whole family sits around Lily's small table and

eats anchovy and pepperoni pizza. Joey sits on a stool way lower than everyone else. They hear MUF-FLED YELLS of an argument through the walls. Lily, embarrassed, gets up to turn on the radio.

MIMMO: See what kind of people live in these places.

LILY: They're just having a little argument.

MIMMO: Yeah sure. Sounds like someone's being killed in there.

MICHELA: Leave her alone.

VINNIE: So where's the bedroom?

Lily points to the futon.

VINNIE: And you're paying how much?

LILY: Shut up Vinnie. It's a nice neighborhood.

MIMMO: We gave you everything and this is where you wanna live like a bum.

Two POLICEMAN pound on Lily's door.

POLICEMAN #1: LAPD open up!

Lily opens her peephole and can barely see anything.

MICHELA: Why is the police here? Did she pay the rent?

POLICEMAN #1: This is the LAPD, I said open up.

MIMMO: Open it up.

Lily opens. The police immediately look inside,

hands on their guns.

POLICEMAN #2: We got a complaint about some noise coming from this apartment.

He motions to Mimmo.

POLICEMAN #2: Sir would you mind coming outside so we can talk?

MIMMO: Who me?

POLICEMAN #1: Yes you. You can either cooperate or we'll have to restrain you.

Michela throws herself in Mimmo's arms.

MICHELA: You leave my husband alone.

LILY: Wait, this must be a misunderstanding.

POLICEMAN #2: It's natural for you to want to protect him, but in America it is against the law to hit your wife.

MIMMO: Hit my wife! She'd kill me with rat poisoning. Who says I hit my wife? Only when she gets out of line ya know.

Mimmo laughs at what he thinks is a funny joke. The police move in to Mimmo and a CRASH and BROKEN GLASS can be heard across the way.

LILY: Excuse me, I think you're looking for apartment 238.

POLICEMAN #1: Oh sorry about that. Have a good night.

The police rush out and BANG on the neighbor's door. Everyone goes back to eating.

MIMMO: Oh yeah, this is a nice neighborhood alright.

They hear COMMOTION from the hallway.

POLICEMAN #1: LAPD open up! That's it we're coming in!

The sound of a door being BUSTED.

LILY: Here let me turn on the radio.

VINNIE: No I wanna hear what happens.

JOEY: This is better than watching cops.

Michela takes out a handkerchief for her tears. Mimmo comforts her.

SAMANTHA: Let go of me! Help!

Lily recognizes Samantha's voice and opens her front door.

INT. APARTMENT BUILDING HALLWAY - CONTINUOUS

Lily walks out and watches as Policeman #1 tries to restrain Samantha while she kicks and screams and Policeman #2 handcuffs Rocko

and his new wife, six foot tall BAMBI (45) dressed in a tight leopard dress with a dolly parton wig - Samantha's parents.

POLICEMAN #1 (to Samantha): Calm down, do you

have a family member or friend you can stay with?

SAMANTHA: No! And I'm not going to a foster home again!

Lily walks out.

LILY: Excuse me. She can stay with me.

Samantha is shocked and calms down.

POLICEMAN #1 (to Samantha): Is she a family friend?

LILY: Oh yeah, we hang out all the time. Right Sammie?

Lily winks at Samantha.

SAMANTHA: Yeah. She's cool.

POLICEMAN #1: Alright then. I'm not gonna call social services and you can stay with your friend for now.

POLICEMAN #2: I want you to know you're gonna be responsible for her. Are you sure about this?

SAMANTHA: I'm gonna be eighteen in two weeks anyway.

LILY: I'm sure. Come on Sammy, we're having pizza.

The policeman lets go of Sammy and she runs into Lily's apartment.

INT. LILY'S APARTMENT - CONTINUOUS

Samantha runs into an unexpected house full of people who all stare at her.

MIMMO (whispers to Michela): She's a midget.

MICHELA: No, you say little person. No midget.

MIMMO: That's not right to make fun of her. She's just a person, how's that.

LILY: Dad, stop it please.

Lily is embarrassed.

VINNIE: How you doing?

Vinnie's eyes light up!

EXT. NOISSAP STREET SIDEWALK - MORNING

Peter walks on the sidewalk in front of Lily's building with two Iced Coffees.

Samantha, clad in her fluorescent pads, zooms out of the parking garage and crashes right into Peter. The coffees spill all over him.

PETER: We meet again.

Samantha picks up her duffel bag and books and gets back on her scooter.

SAMANTHA: I'm sorry.

PETER: You did that on purpose right?

SAMANTHA: No, it was an accident.

Peter is surprised by her new behavior.

SAMANTHA: I'm supposed to wear glasses and I can't see very well.

PETER: Hey it's okay, don't worry about it.

Samantha zooms off for school. Peter is confused.

INT. APARTMENT - LATER

Lily makes homemade iced coffee for her and Peter. She joins him on the bean bag. The room is bright and the sun shines on them.

LILY: Mine's better than starbucks anyway.

PETER: Thanks Lil.

They sip coffee in a comfortable silence.

LILY: Ever since we met, my world has been chaos, but I don't even feel stressed about it.

PETER: Sometimes circumstances are just out of our control. I actually have some good news.

LILY: Really? What?!

PETER: We got our first gig at the Roxy on Monday night!

LILY: No way, that's great! I'm gonna have to kick some groupie's ass.

PETER: About that. You have nothing to worry about.

LILY: Yeah I better not or you'll have to deal with my Italian temper.

They laugh playfully.

PETER: Wow that sounds pretty tempting. I bet you're hot even when you're mad.

LILY: Well don't test me.

PETER: Never.

Lily grabs his coffee and sets them down on the floor. She takes off her shirt and unbuttons his.

PETER: I like a girl who knows what she wants.

LILY: Any girl? Or just me?

PETER: Just you. Ever since the minute I saw you.

Peter finishes taking off his shirt as Lily slips her blouse up over her head revealing a sexy black bra. He pulls her toward him and they passionately kiss. Peter is almost afraid to touch her. He slowly moves to the back of her bra.

PETER: Is it okay?

LILY: Hold on.

Lily gets up and disappears into the other room for a minute. Peter is not sure what's going on but he's happy. "You Belong to Me" begins to play softly. Lily shows up in the doorway with absolutely nothing on and her hair pulled up. Peter is pleasantly surprised. She pulls off her eye patch.

LILY: My eye's all better now.

PETER: I'm speechless.

Peter walks over to Lily and she wraps her legs around his waist as they get intimate.

EXT. BEACH BOARDWALK - DAY

Samantha and Lily, head to toe in pads, skate along the boardwalk. Lily doesn't skate well, but Samantha's a pro.

LILY: You know, I have to confess that I used to think you were a total bitch.

SAMANTHA: And I used to think you were a stuck up, drama queen who cried just because the world didn't bow down to you.

LILY: Wow, let's not hold anything back.

SAMANTHA: Well how could you possibly have anything to worry about in life?

LILY: Trust me, everything that can go wrong does go wrong.

Lily falls flat on her ass.

SAMANTHA: Maybe in your narcissistic mind.

LILY: I don't appreciate that. For your information, my problems are very real. You can ask my mom.

Samantha zooms around Lily as she nurses her knee on a bench.

SAMANTHA: Why would I do that?

LILY: Cause she would tell you that I've been cursed

since birth.

SAMANTHA: What do you mean cursed?

LILY: I mean a witch in Italy put a spell on me.

SAMANTHA: Oh right, and I'm in the lollipop guild?

LILY: That's not funny. Okay it's a little funny.

The girls LAUGH.

LILY: You don't believe me, but I'm not kidding.

SAMANTHA: Don't be so naive. There is no such thing as witches and spells.

LILY: Yes there is and my family is from a town called Benevento where many Italian witches live.

SAMANTHA: There's no such thing as witches.

LILY: Yeah there is.

Samantha has a seat next to Lily.

SAMANTHA: I was right. You are a drama queen and you have no idea what it's like to have real problems. How would you like growing up with six different step moms. And then have to watch each one leave because of my abusive father.

LILY: Samantha I'm sorry.

SAMANTHA: Why are you sorry? There's nothing to be sorry about. What you need to do is stop focusing on all of the bad things that happen to you. You're not a victim and you control your own destiny.

LILY: You really believe that?

SAMANTHA: Yes. I learned it from a meme on twitter.

LILY: I only get the pessimistic memes in my feed. Aren't I supposed to be the one trying to make you feel better? I'm technically your mom.

SAMANTHA: You're four years older than me.

LILY: I still believe there's a curse on me.

A seagull flies by and POOPS right on top of Lily's head.

LILY: See it's a sign from God! This happens all the time.

SAMANTHA: Okay, let's say you really are hexed. Why don't you go to another witch and tell her to reverse it.

LILY: Hmmm I wonder if that would work.

Lily grabs a bandana from her hair and uses it to try to wipe to bird poop out of her hair.

SAMANTHA: Well since witches are real and so are spells, then I'm sure there's got to be a way to magically reverse it.

LILY: Okay. So maybe I will. Maybe all I've ever needed to do is go back to Italy and find a witch.

SAMANTHA: I know a place in Studio City. That might be easier.

A stranger hands Lily a flyer. Lily looks at it and rolls her eyes at the tropicali bathing suit contest.

LILY: Oh god. I am not gonna do a stupid swimsuit contest.

SAMANTHA: Why not. With those melons you'll probably win.

LILY: It has taken me a long time to feel comfortable with these but not comfortable enough to walk across a stage in a bikini top.

SAMANTHA: I wish I could do it.

LILY: Samantha, you have a great figure. If you want to do it, you should. You know what, I'll do it with you fuck it.

SAMANTHA: No way.

LILY: Yes way. We're gonna be in this contest and be proud of our bodies.

SAMANTHA: I don't think I could handle anyone making fun of me.

A douche ROLLERBLADER man in his 40s zooms by.

ROLLERBLADER: Nice tits!!

SAMANTHA: Fuck off loser!

LILY: I've had to deal with DDD boobs since 7th grade so I know what it feels like to have unwanted attention. Let's be each other's moral support. You are gorgeous and I promise no one will say a word or

I'll personally make a few phone calls to take care of them if you know what I mean.

SAMANTHA: Okay fine I'll do it. But just so you know, that whole whoa is me and my big boobs speech has got to go. No one is going to feel sorry for you for having giant tits. Okay mafia girl?

LILY: See now you're making assumptions. Just because I'm Italian doesn't mean that.

SAMANTHA: Yeah whatever. I met your family.

LILY: Oh shoot I gotta go. I'm meeting Peter at his place and he's making lunch.

SAMANTHA: I wish I had a childhood sweetheart. You guys are cute.

LILY: We aren't childhood sweethearts. We literally just met 2 weeks ago. But I'm obsessed with him.

SAMANTHA: What? No way! Maybe there's hope for me.

LILY: Of course there is! You're only 17! I'll see you back at the apartment.

SAMANTHA: Okay don't be late tonight!

LILY: I won't. See you later.

Lily wobbles away on skates as Samantha looks at the flyer and smiles. Another old leather skin man skates by and WHISTLES at Samantha.

SAMANTHA: Okay boomer! You're disgusting.

INT. PETER'S APARTMENT - DAY

Lily and Peter sit on floor pillows with empty plates on the coffee table. Gorgeous city views below from floor to ceiling windows.

LILY: So I'm doing this tropical swimwear contest with Samantha tonight and I was wondering if you could come out. She is really nervous and I just want to support her.

PETER: Absolutely! That's sweet of you.

LILY: My brothers are going to be there and they are just sometimes loud and embarrassing and I don't want to scare you away.

PETER: You don't have to worry at all. I'm sure they are great. Plus you survived my crazy family.

LILY: But mine is crazy in a different way.

PETER: Imagine holidays? I can't stop thinking about you.

LILY: Good. Thank you for lunch. I love scallops.

PETER: I think I love you. I know it's soon but this is crazy. It was love at first sight.

LILY (giggles): I'm falling very hard for you but I don't think we should say it unless we mean it.

PETER: Okay deal. I don't think I'm going to change my mind but I'll wait.

LILY: I have an interview tomorrow at Strego's. I

really hope I get it because I don't want to have to work for my parent's restaurant. I know they are waiting for me to fail so I'll go back home.

PETER: Oh you'll get it for sure. I actually have some good news too. My band just submitted our demo to the whisky on sunset.

LILY: That's amazing!! When do you find out?

PETER: I don't know. My parents are really on me about college so I hope I get it just to prove that I'm going to be okay doing music. We rehearse 5 hours almost every day and the rest of the time I'm writing lyrics, but they just want me to work in finance like my dad.

LILY: It's your life and I think you should do what makes you happy.

They kiss.

PETER: Listen, I was thinking...

LILY: Yeah, thinking what?

PETER: I thought that maybe it would be nice if you spent the night after the contest tonight?

LILY: And wake up in each other's arms again but maybe naked this time.

PETER: Yes.

LILY: That sounds nice.

CUT TO:

INT. THE FRITZ HOTEL BANQUET ROOM - EVENING

Ten bathing suit models are lined up on stage. Lily and Samantha stand next to each other. An AN-NOUNCER stands at one side of the stage with a microphone and envelope in his hand. Balloons are everywhere and camera flashes illuminate the stage. Lily's brothers and Peter are in the crowd.

ANNOUNCER: Let's take one last look at these gorgeous ladies before we announce the winners.

Upbeat MUSIC shakes the crowd as each of the girls make their way down the runway. Samantha looks great in a yellow one piece and the crowd CHEERS. Samantha turns around and starts twerking and the crowd goes WILD. Lily tries to dance too but doesn't dance as well.

VINNIE: I don't care what you say, she is hot!

JOEY: Come on Vinnie, leave this one alone.

VINNIE: What, she's just a regular girl like everyone else.

JOEY: Yeah, but you fuck over everyone else. Come on, Lily's trying to help her get her life together.

VINNIE: Lily barely has her own life together first of all. And what's your problem, you're a sick bastard if you think I would just use her.

JOEY: What's your problem? Why wouldn't I think that? That's what you always do.

VINNIE: Be quiet, here comes Lily.

Lily comes down the stage in a gorgeous blue floral bikini with beads hanging down at the ties. She wears a band aid from her skating accident earlier. Joey and Vinnie CHEER and WHISTLE.

JOEY: Yeah that's my sister!

Lily smiles at Peter. She suddenly loses her balance, trips and falls off the edge of the stage. The crowd catches her fall. The crowd GASPS.

ANNOUNCER: Help her up is she okay?

Lily, embarrassed, stands up.

LILY: I'm okay.

She walks backstage as some people laugh. A GUY close to Vinnie is one of them.

VINNIE: Hey you gotta problem?

GUY: No no problem. Sorry man.

VINNIE: Yeah you better be!

ANNOUNCER: And now for the second runner up - Bobby from Venice Beach.

Crowd CHEERS. Peter looks concerned.

ANNOUNCER: The first runner up is SAMANTHA MARLOW from Sherman Oaks!

Vinnie begins jumping up and down. He realizes Joey is staring at him so he stops.

INT. BACKSTAGE - MOMENTS LATER

Lily and Samantha are hugging. A TRENDY WOMAN (40s) approaches them.

TRENDY WOMAN: Excuse me. Samantha?

SAMANTHA: Yes, hi.

TRENDY WOMAN: Hi. I'm the producer of a T.V. show called LA Babes, have you heard of it?

SAMANTHA (excited): Yes I have!

TRENDY WOMAN: I'd love to have you join our cast.

SAMANTHA: Really?!

TRENDY WOMAN: We have a super diverse cast lined up and I believe it is fate that I happened to find you here.

Samantha hugs the Trendy Woman.

LILY: Do you have a card or something?

TRENDY WOMAN: Oh yes of course. She pulls out a press badge and business card.

LILY: Cool. Just looking out for my best friend.

A SHADY MAN walks up to Lily and interrupts. Samantha continues to talk to the Trendy Woman.

SHADY MAN: Hi there. I'm Mr. Slowensky.

LILY (snooty): Yes. Can I help you?

He hands her a card.

SHADY MAN: I'm from Penthouse magazine and I'd like to do a test shoot with you to be considered for our next Pet of the Month.

LILY: You've got the wrong girl.

SHADY MAN: We're talking $20,000 just for some topless shots and 50 gees if you show us all the goods. Change your mind now?

LILY: I'll have to think about it.

SHADY MAN: Yes, of course. Take your time. Just get back to me by the first.

LILY: Okay, sounds good.

The Shady Man walks away. Lily puts the card in her purse.

EXT. NOISSAP STREET SIDEWALK - EVENING

Peter and Lily are bundled up in beanies and coats. The Santa Ana winds blow. They walk hand in hand.

PETER: That's really great about Samantha. You sure you're okay?

LILY: I'm totally fine. Only in LA. She leaves next week on her birthday to film for 6 months.

PETER: That's crazy.

LILY: Something else crazy happened. A man gave me his card and said he wants me to pose for penthouse.

PETER: If you want to do it, go for it. I'll back you up no matter what.

LILY: He said they pay like twenty grand. I don't really want to do it, but I'm saving the card just in case.

PETER: I know you will get something soon. I would be happier if you did it because you want to and not because you feel like you need to.

LILY: Yeah I know. I don't even know if I really want to act anymore. I love getting lost in characters but maybe it's because I'm trying to always escape myself.

PETER: I get that because music is my escape. The good thing is you don't need to make all of these decisions in one night and you can change your mind anytime. The world is yours Lily and I want to support you in whatever you do. Do you want me to come up?

LILY: I want you to, but there's just not much space in my apartment and I need to wake up early for another interview.

PETER: Totally understand. I'll see you tomorrow?

LILY: Yeah.

They kiss goodbye.

INT. APARTMENT - MOMENTS LATER

TOP GUN plays on the T.V. as Samantha and Vinnie lay on the futon and kiss. Lily opens the front door and walks in on them.

LILY: Oh my god! Vinnie get off her!

Vinnie and Samantha jump up in embarrassment.

SAMANTHA: Hey Lily, it's okay.

Lily goes and SLAPS Vinnie in the face.

LILY: You pig!

VINNIE: What? Leave me alone.

LILY: Tell me this isn't happening. What the hell do you two think you are doing? And on my bed, ew get off!

SAMANTHA: We are two teenagers making out!

LILY: Samantha, no offense, but this is my brother and you deserve someone much nicer.

VINNIE: Jesus tell us how you really feel.

LILY: You! I don't want to hear another word from you. You're a slob!

VINNIE: It's not like that I swear.

SAMANTHA (to Lily): I think this is my choice not yours.

VINNIE: Lily, We have been texting since that first night and we like each other.

LILY: Vinnie just get out of here please.

SAMANTHA: You really are a self-centered bitch! If he's leaving so am I.

LILY: Fine!

VINNIE AND SAMANTHA: Fine!

Vinnie and Samantha storm out of the apartment. As they walk out, Nina walks in.

NINA: Knock knock neighbor.

LILY: Oh hi, I'm just going to bed.

NINA: Come on. What's bothering you?

LILY: Nothing.

NINA: I'm going to cheer you right up. I'll be right back.

Nina runs out. Lily gives up and throws herself on the beanbag. Nina comes back with a big bowl of rum cake (with extra rum), strawberries and whip cream.

NINA: Here eat this and you'll feel much better.

Lily pathetically takes a bite and actually likes it as usual.

LILY: Wow, this is just like my mom's rum cake.

NINA: See I knew you'd like it. I googled Italian desserts and wanted to surprise you. Now give me the tea, what's going on with you?

LILY: Nothing really.

NINA: Come on I promise not to tell anyone else in the building or my church. Of course I'll tell Brad. I tell him everything.

LILY: Just had a rough day that's all.

Lily starts to feel dizzy.

LILY: Wow, there's a lot of rum in there.

NINA (smiling): Yeah and just a touch of absinthe. That's my secret ingredient.

LILY: Isn't that illegal?

NINA: Well it is in America, but we smuggled this from Amsterdam.

LILY: Uh oh, I don't handle alcohol well.

Lily feels light-headed.

NINA: Don't worry, I'll take care of you. Why don't I give you a facial. I used to be an esthetician.

LILY (drunkenly): Sure, I'll have a facial.

INT. BATHROOM - MOMENTS LATER

Lily sits on the toilet as Nina rubs a thick green mask all over her face. SPA MUSIC plays with rain and gong sounds. Lily is wasted.

INT. APARTMENT -- MORNING

Lily lays asleep in a white robe and cucumbers on her

eyes. She sits up and the cucumbers fall off. She holds her head as it aches. The CLOCK reads 10:00AM.

LILY: Shit. I missed the fucking interview.

Lily touches her face and it has a bright red rash all over it. She grabs a small mirror off a table and looks.

LILY: Oh my god! What did she do to me!

Nina POUNDS on the front door.

NINA (O.S.): Rise and shine. I brought you some Turkish coffee.

LILY: No! I mean...Peter's here. Peter, hold on a second.

NINA (O.S.): I won't judge a booty call.

Lily hears a key in the doorknob. She dashes to the door and props a chair under it.

LILY: Not right now. We're not dressed.

LILY (to herself): She's clinically insane.

INT. LILY'S PARENT'S HOUSE - AFTERNOON

Lots of plants and fake flowers. The white couches have plastic. Lily's whole family, Samantha and Peter all sit together at a round table with a checkered tablecloth. A big bowl of Spaghetti is in the center along with many side dishes. Lily's cheeks are still a bit red from the mask.

VINNIE: Ma, Dad, me and Samantha are getting married. Not right away, but when she gets back from filming. We'll both be 18.

LILY: You're what? You've only known each other for two weeks.

SAMANTHA: Actually it's been 16 days.

MICHELA: Oh that's nice.

MIMMO: Finally we'll get some grandchildren. Uh oh... Are yous pregnant?

VINNIE: No, it's not like that. We're in love and we wanna get married young and have a family like you and ma.

Michela does the sign of the cross. She's happy.

JOEY: Congrats brother. I've never seen you like this.

LILY: You're too young.

Peter stays out of the conversation and is the only one eating spaghetti.

MIMMO: Congratulations and welcome to the family Samantha. I guess we're gonna have a movie star in the family. Lily, you could've been too. Why didn't you pose in that magazine?

LILY: You wanted me to pose in penthouse? Thanks dad.

MIMMO: Well so what. It could've been a stepping stone to other things.

MICHELA: Sophia Loren was naked in her first film and look at her now.

Peter stuffs his mouth and avoids eye contact.

LILY: That's disgusting. I'm not going to take off my clothes for a sick magazine. I'm going to college. Who said I want to be a model.

MIMMO: Model Actress same thing.

LILY: Nevermind about me. Samantha if this is what you really want, then of course I support it.

SAMANTHA: Thank you.

Everyone begins to dig in.

MIMMO: Here Peter have some more.

He puts a giant heap of spaghetti in his plate.

PETER: Thanks Mr. DeVito.

MICHELA: So what nationality are you Peter?

PETER: I'm part Irish and part Italian.

MIMMO: You know them Irish, they like to drink. How about some wine?

Peter politely laughs.

MICHELA: Where were you born?

PETER: In California.

MIMMO: I could tell.

PETER: Oh really.

MIMMO: You guys in California are just more delicate than the guys back east. You know with the earrings and the bracelets. You wouldn't be caught dead wearing that where I grew up. If you weren't wearing black shiny boots and a belt to match with a white T-shirt and greased up hair, you'd get your ass kicked. You wouldn't last a day back east.

Peter doesn't respond and tries to laugh it off. Everyone starts talking over each other.

LILY: Dad will you stop already. No one acts like that anymore. We are gen z.

MICHELA: Why don't you shut up and eat Mimmo.

VINNIE (whispers to Peter): You fuck over my sister and you're a dead man you understand?

MIMMO: Why are you always busting my balls, we had style back then. None of this sissy stuff.

PETER: I would never hurt your sister. You don't have to worry.

MICHELA: Watch your mouth.

VINNIE: Consider yourself warned.

Lily stands up and starts to clear dishes.

LILY: I didn't know about Vinnie's news tonight, but Peter and I have some news too.

PETER: If it's okay with you Mr. and Mrs. DeVito, Lily and I would like to move in together.

MIMMO: You're what?!

LILY: Ma, come on you understand. Times are different.

MICHELA: What have I always taught you? If you give him the milk for free, he's never gonna buy the cow.

MIMMO: Sorry to disappoint you, but you're not moving in with him and that's the end of the story.

LILY: Yes I am.

MIMMO (yells): Over my dead body!

MIMMO (to Peter): You come in my house and then tell me you wanna move in with my daughter, you can go to hell!

Peter is frightened.

PETER: I'm sorry you feel that way. Thank you for dinner. I'm going to get going.

LILY: I'm coming with you. This is not your decision ma, dad. This is ours.

Michela does the sign of the cross again but upset.

INT. PETER'S CONVERTIBLE MERCEDES - LATER

PETER: I don't know Lily, your dad sounded pretty serious.

LILY: He's all talk, I promise.

Peter pulls into a spot at the top of Mulholland drive and turns off the car.

LILY: It's beautiful up here.

PETER: Look, I am going to be with you no matter

what. None of this is gonna scare me away. I know this has been a crazy day, but I have something to tell you.

LILY: Oh no, what's wrong?

PETER: It's fine. It's just, my parents told me that I'm getting cut off financially if I don't go back to school.

LILY: I'm so sorry.

PETER: That includes my apartment. I know it's silly because most people have to pay their own rent anyway, but I actually wanted to ask you if we could share your place. The rent is way cheaper than mine and we can share the rent and focus on what we really want to do without worrying.

LILY: I mean we can meet in the middle and get something a bit nicer.

PETER: I love your place and as long as we can be together, I don't care where we live.

LILY: You really want to move in with me.

PETER: I really do. I told you from the beginning, I don't want our crazy families to get in our way. I love you.

LILY: You do?

PETER: I have loved you and it's stronger every day.

LILY: I love you too. God that's so scary to say.

PETER: I know. Let's figure this life out together.

LILY: I would love that. I have something for you.

Lily gets up and grabs the Mickey and Minnie Heart Keychain out of her purse and hands it to Peter.

PETER: Ha amazing! It's really mine this time.

LILY: You don't have to keep it on the Mickey keychain though.

PETER: But this one is so cool. I can't wait to wake up every day with you.

LILY: Me too babe. I have something I wanted to tell you.

PETER: What else you got?

LILY: Samantha put me on the waitlist for some celebrity witch in Studio City who can apparently break curses.

Peter and Lily laugh together.

PETER: When are you going?

LILY: Tomorrow!

PETER: Oh I wish I could be there, I promised nana I'd take her to her favorite restaurant Inn of the Seventh Ray.

LILY: No, go and tell her I say hi. I'll let you know how it goes.

They put their seats back, hold hands and look up at the stars.

INT. PSYCHIC EYE - DAY

Lily walks through some beads into a fortune teller cove and has a seat. JEZEBEL (long gray hair, 50s) looks stone faced and doesn't say anything just motions for Lily to pick a card.

Jezebel turns over the HANGED MAN.

JEZEBEL: What brings you here today ma'am.

LILY: Well, this sounds silly but...

JEZEBEL: Somebody put a hex on you?

LILY (tears up): Yes. Can you tell?

JEZEBEL: Yes. This is strong. Hold my hand.

Jezebel closes her eyes and rocks back and forth. She begins saying prayers in another language. She then reaches into a drawer and takes out a mother Teresa bottle that holds holy water. She splashes some at Lily's face.

JEZEBEL: The hanged man means the tides will turn for you. The first half has been how do you say, accident prone, bad luck. The second half of life is good. But only if the hex is removed.

LILY: Okay, how is it removed?

Jezebel reaches down to a cupboard and pulls out a very large candle.

JEZEBEL: This candle needs to be lit for three days and I will do a spell each night. At the end of the three days, the curse will be broken.

LILY: Okay. Sounds good. How much is the candle?

JEZEBEL: $100.

LILY: Okay, well I have a credit card.

Lily digs for it in her bag and hands it over. Jezebel's eyes pop out and she stops.

JEZEBEL: My child, you got the job. Check your phone.

Lily a little freaked out, takes her phone out of the bag and sure enough she has an email with a start date.

JEZEBEL: The powers are at work.

LILY: How did you know that?

Jezebel snaps out of it and hands back her credit card and circles the tip line.

JEZEBEL: I'm a witch. Do you believe in me?

LILY: Yes.

Lily filled out a $20 tip.

LILY: Okay, well that's all I really needed. Is there anything else I need to do besides light the candle?

JEZEBEL: The candle is not for you. I need to light it every night for three days while I do my spell.

LILY: Wait. I just paid for a candle but I don't get to take it.

JEZEBEL: No! On the third day, fill a glass bowl with water, dip your middle finger in olive oil and drop three drops of oil into the water. If the drops stay on top of the water, the curse has been removed. If the oil drops to the bottom, it didn't work.

Jezebel motions for her to leave.

LILY: Thank you very much.

JEZEBEL: One more thing. Splash warm water on your face three times when you get home.

EXT. SIDEWALK - MOMENTS LATER

Lily is on her phone with Samantha

LILY: I don't know it was so weird. I got a job at a law firm and she knew! She told me to look at my phone and then she sold me a candle to break the spell but I wasn't allowed to take the candle with me.

SAMANTHA (O.S.): Wow that sounds fun. That's amazing that she knew. Also congrats!

LILY: I know! Thank you. So after that I just handed her $100.

SAMANTHA (O.S.): I would too. Take my money you witch.

INT. LILY'S BATHROOM - LATER

Lily splashes water on her face three times and dries it off with a soft yellow towel. She feels good.

Peter CALLS and she answers in the bathroom while

doing her skincare routine.

PETER (O.S.): How did it go?

LILY: I'll give you details later, but it was so weird and I got a job!

PETER: At the restaurant? That's great!

LILY: No I sent off my resume to an agency for a part time job at a law firm and I didn't think I had a chance but they want me to start tomorrow. And get this, the witch knew I got it. She told me to check my phone and she was right.

PETER (O.S.): No way! Maybe this is all real.

LILY: I told you it's real!

PETER: I'm so happy for you babe. I'm almost done with lunch and then I'll start packing. Are you okay with using some of my furniture and I'll put what doesn't fit in storage.

LILY: Absolutely. Mine is all hand me downs. Samantha is leaving on Saturday, so you can move in anytime after that.

PETER: Great. I'm so excited. Love you.

LILY: Love you too.

Lily sets down her phone, walks out to the living room/bedroom area, gets the Penthouse business card out of her purse and tears it up. Phone RINGS.

LILY: Hey Sam what's up?

SAMANTHA (O.S.): Vinnie and I are going to the Gauntlet to celebrate my birthday and farewell party. Can you and Peter come out tomorrow.

LILY: Peter has rehearsal, but I'll be there.

SAMANTHA: Okay great.

INT. THE GAUNTLET CLUB - EVENING

Samantha wears a birthday crown and Vinnie, Joey and Lily dance to heavy TRANCE MUSIC. The crowd is mainly goth with a few questionable characters.

LILY: I'm gonna go get a drink, does anyone want anything?

SAMANTHA: Water please girl.

VINNIE: Let me have some of your drink.

LILY: No Vinnie, you're only 17.

VINNIEL: Fine, a water.

JOEY: Same.

Lily goes through the crowd to the bar. She waves down the bartender.

LILY: Hi can I get 3 waters and a vodka tonic with 3 limes.

BARTENDER: Sure beautiful.

The bartender puts the cocktail in front of her and she sips it while he gets the waters. The bartender re-fills her cocktail with extra vodka and winks at her.

LILY: Thanks.

Lily gets a TEXT from Samantha: WHAT'S TAKING SO LONG? FORGET THE DRINKS AND MEET US AT BREWHOUSE NEXT DOOR.

Lily TEXTS back: OKAY I'M JUST GOING TO FINISH MY DRINK AND I'LL BE THERE.

As Lily looks down at her phone, a vampire type guy puts something in her drink and walks away. Lily misses it and finishes her drink then drinks some of the water. She makes her way to the bathroom.

INT. GAUNTLETT BATHROOM - MOMENTS LATER

Lily goes into the bathroom and chooses the handicap stall at the end. She starts to feel the effects of the drug. The room spins. She locks the door and falls to the floor. Her phone in hand she dials Vinnie's cell. No answer. She tries Samantha. No answer. She dials Peter.

CUT TO:

INT. MUSIC STUDIO - CONTINUOUS

Peter and his band rehearses. Peter is in the middle, plays guitar. He sees his phone light up on the amp. Stops playing and picks up.

PETER: One second guys. Hi babe, having fun?

CUT TO:

INT. GAUNTLET BATHROOM - CONTINUOUS

Lily is in the fetal position, tears stream down.

LILY: I'm...

PETER (O.S.): Lily, baby, what's wrong?

LILY: I had a drink... it wasn't good.

PETER: Where are you?

LILY: I'm in the bathroom stall.

Lily begins to cry. Women outside the stall TALK LOUD and can't hear Lily over the music.

PETER: Where are you babe?

LILY: The Gauntlet.

PETER: Listen to me. Don't go anywhere. You understand me. I'm ten minutes away and I'm leaving right now.

LILY: Okay.

PETER: I love you baby. Just stay right there.

EXT. PARKING LOT - CONTINUOUS

Peter runs to his car and takes off.

INT. GAUNTLET BATHROOM - MOMENTS LATER

Lily lays her face on the ground next to the toilet and closes her eyes. Moments later, Peter rushes into the bathroom.

PETER: Lily?!

No answer. Peter looks under and sees Lily.

PETER: Lil, open the door babe.

LILY: I can't.

PETER: Okay. That's okay. I'm gonna crawl under.

Peter lays on the ground and army crawls under the stall. He scoops her up into his lap and wipes her hair and drool off her face.

PETER: What happened babe? Let's get you out of here.

Peter scoops her up.

LILY: I don't know. Everyone left and I was finishing my drink and then I came to the bathroom and I'm sick.

Peter can hardly understand her. He kicks open the bathroom door.

INT. GAUNTLET - CONTINUOUS

Peter makes his way through the club with Lily in his arms. CLUB GOERS stare as they go by.

CLUB GOER #1: What's the matter with her?

CLUB GOER #2 (laughs): Party foul.

INT. HOSPITAL ROOM - LATER

Lily's whole family, Samantha and Peter surround a sleeping Lily in the bed. Dr. Ronald walks in with his clipboard.

DR. RONALD: It looks like someone slipped a xanax

into her drink. Sometimes this can be used to relax on a date.

Everyone looks at the doctor.

MIMMO: What did you just say? I told you Michela, this guy has some screws loose.

Peter PUNCHES Dr. Ronald. Vinnie and Joey are impressed. Mimmo holds Peter back.

MIMMO (to doctor): Get the hell out of here. You creepy fuck. I never want to see you around anyone in my family again.

DR. RONALD: I'm sorry Mr. DeVito. I'm leaving. I'll send in someone else.

Dr. Ronald stumbles out.

PETER: I'm sorry. I've never gotten into a fight in my life.

MIMMO (tears stream): That guy had it coming. You saved my daughter's life. She coulda been raped or even killed and you saved her.

Michela comforts Mimmo and takes her daughter's hand.

PETER: I would do anything for your daughter sir.

MIMMO: I made a mistake about you. You're a good guy.

PETER: It's okay. I can understand how you would want to protect her. She's really special.

MIMMO: Okay, it's getting late. Are you gonna stay with her?

PETER: Yes sir. I'm not leaving her side.

MICHELA: Alright let's go.

Mimmo gives Peter a long, hard hug. Michela pinches his cheeks hard and kisses him. Joey and Vinnie both shake his hand and hit his arm. Samantha hugs him.

INT. LILY'S APARTMENT - DAY

Lily in overalls and a white bandana with hair up and Peter in shorts and a t-shirt set down a beautiful couch on a fluffy new rug. Moving day. Peter's queen sized bed is off to the side and a bar top table is snug near the kitchen. The apartment looks so different. Artwork leans against the wall on the floor.

LILY: Wow! I can't believe it all fits.

PETER: It looks great!

They plop down on the couch proud of their home.

LILY: And you know what the best part is?

PETER: What's that?

LILY: It's all ours. And we don't have to answer to my parents or yours anymore.

PETER: That is the best part.

LILY: Oh my god, I almost forgot. I need to do the olive oil thing the witch told me about.

PETER: Absolutely, let's do it.

Lily grabs a clear bowl and fills up with water. Peter hands her the olive oil.

LILY: She told me I need to dip my finger in the oil and put three drops into the bowl.

Peter grabs a ramekin and pours some oil into it.

PETER: Here you go.

Lily dabs her finger into the oil and let's it drop into the water. The drops float and make rings.

LILY: It's floating! That means the curse is broken!

Lily jumps onto Peter and they kiss.

PETER: The curse is broken.

LILY: I don't even care if it's fake. I want to believe.

PETER: For sure.

LILY: Let's celebrate! I had Vinnie and Joey set up a little surprise.

PETER: I love surprises.

LILY: Okay ready? Close your eyes.

Peter closes them and she brings him to the sliding glass door where the patio is. She begins to open the curtains. A small inflatable pool is on the patio.

LILY: Okay open!

PETER: No way! I love it!

EXT. PATIO - LATER

Peter and Lily sit in the inflatable pool with their suits on, sunglasses and sip lemonade.

LILY: I know it's not a penthouse apartment, but I love it here.

PETER: I told you none of that matters to me. This is one of the best days of my life.

LILY: I'm really sorry about the Whisky.

PETER: It's kind of weird but I don't even care. And I actually have something I've been wanting to tell you.

LILY: What's that?

PETER: I'm going back to school too. I've always been really passionate about architecture so I enrolled at ivc to work on my gen ed.

LILY: Really that's awesome! What about the band?

PETER: We are still going to perform, but my drummer is having a baby so it just seems like the right time to pursue other things.

LILY: Speaking of that. I'm not going to act anymore. I just realized that I spent most of my life trying to escape who I am and where I came from. It was so easy to get lost in other characters. And for the first time in my life, I want to be me and it feels like that is enough. Plus I'll never get through college if I continue auditioning.

PETER: Well maybe we are just growing up.

LILY: Yeah. I like it.

PETER: I like you.

They share a smooch.

MONTAGE:

Samantha in heart pink sunglasses on a reality show poster.

Vinnie and Samantha meet at an airport gate and embrace.

Lily and Peter ride bikes on a college campus.

Lily studies law books with glasses and hair up.

Peter works on a house blueprint in the apartment.

Lily and Peter laugh on the couch watching a movie.

Mimmo and Michela and Joey eat at the dinner table with two empty chairs.

Henry kisses Sophia on their yacht while Catherine sips on a cocktail and watches soaps on an iPad.

INT. BANQUET HALL - EVENING

Vinnie and Samantha's wedding reception. It's a Grease themed wedding. An extravagantly decorated but small room with streamers and balloons and flowers in shades of yellow. An Italian couple drops an envelope into a basket in the back of the room. A slick DJ (25 Indian) stands behind turntables with a microphone. Lily's family, Peter and some of Vinnie and Samantha's friends fill three round tables. A small but vibrant crowd. The D.J. stands in the middle of the dance floor.

DJ (Indian Accent): And now for the first time ever, let me introduce Mr. And Mrs. Vinnie and Samantha DeVito!

Everyone jumps to their feet and cheers. A couple DWARVES stand on their chairs and WHISTLE. Vinnie has slicked hair in a black tux and Samantha is in a beaded white gown. Her train is very long and two of her friends hold it up for her.

DJ: Now Vinnie and Samantha will lead us into our first dance.

The D.J. plays the song from STAYING ALIVE. Vinnie and Samantha do a planned dance.

DJ: Come on let's get this party started. Everyone to the dance floor.

Lily and Peter laugh and get up and hit the dance floor. Mimmo grabs Michela's hand and she pulls away.

MIMMO: Come on, let's show them how we danced in Rome.

MICHELA: You haven't danced with me in twenty years and now I don't wanna dance.

MIMMO: Come on. It's a wedding, you're supposed to dance. It's gonna look funny if we don't dance.

MICHELA: Okay, let's dance.

Mimmo and Michela hit the floor and start busting out some really old moves. They are both really into it. Lily and Peter are laughing at all of the crazy dancers around them. The dwarf couples are getting down to the disco music as well. Peter spins Lily around and she trips on an extension cord. She throws her arms up in the air to catch her balance and Peter loses his grip on her. Lily falls right into the beautiful tiered wedding cake. The room GASPS. Samantha walks up to Lily with her hands on her hip. Lily lays on the floor and looks up at her.

LILY: Oops.

SAMANTHA: Girl you aren't cursed, you are clumsy as fuck.

Everyone LAUGHS. Peter lends his hand and helps Lily to her feet. Everyone continues to dance.

PETER: Do we need to go back to the witch?

LILY: She stole my candle!

They LAUGH. Lily wipes the cake out of her hair and face and takes a lick.

LILY: Mmm. It's good.

PETER: Let me taste.

Peter kisses Lily's lips gently. "You're the One That I Want" from GREASE comes on. Joey wears "greaser" clothes and slides through the middle of the dance floor on his knees. Samantha and Vinnie come out in costumes that Olivia Newton John and John Travolta wore and reenact the scene while everyone dances around them. Two doves fly circles around the room. We watch the party from the dove's POV. The doves fly out a small window. Their silhouettes can be seen in the full moon. An accordion upbeat Italian song plays as the credits roll over the moon.

FADE OUT.